Magical Stories for Magical Kids!

We are a Fair Trade Publishing company; the first of its kind. Meaning, we value the artists we work with, which is why we pay them 3x more than traditional publishing. When you buy our books & subscription, you support these hard-working, creative humans to inspire your kids. Thank you!

To the adventurous spirit within each of us. May we always continue to stay curious and be bold enough to explore what's on the other side!

-Bradley

To Mama, Papa, and Amma.

-Sauryn

For all the inquisitive explorers!

-Amy

ISBN: 978-1-990568-10-7 (Paperback)
ISBN: 978-1-990568-11-4 (Hardcover)

Written By: Bradley T. Morris
Illustrated By: Amy Ebrahimian
Book Design By: Sarah Van Alstyne
Edited By: Emily Williams

Printed by IngramSpark, Inc., in the United States of America.
First printing edition 2021
IngramSpark
14 Ingram Blvd,
La Vergne, TN
37086,
United States

www.MajikKids.com

The Other Side:
The Untold Story of why the Chicken REALLY Crossed the Road

Bradley T. Morris & Sauryn Majik
Illustrated By Amy Ebrahimian

We have all heard the age-old question, "Why did the chicken cross the road?" But have you ever wondered what drew that curious chicken to the other side?

Well, our team of Children's Story Investigative Researchers wanted to know the truth behind the chicken and so we set out to find the answers to the questions most of us have been wondering our entire lives.

Questions like:

- Why did the chicken REALLY cross the road?
- Why would she leave her family, friends, food, farm and security?
- And what did she do when she got to the other side?

We were fortunate enough to catch up with Old MacDonald, who was the farmer who raised the Chicken that crossed the road. This story is based on the old, fuzzy memories stored inside his noodle noggin – the technical term used to describe "his head."

So here we go with our historical interview with Old MacDonald, finally explaining: **WHY DID THE CHICKEN CROSS THE ROAD?**

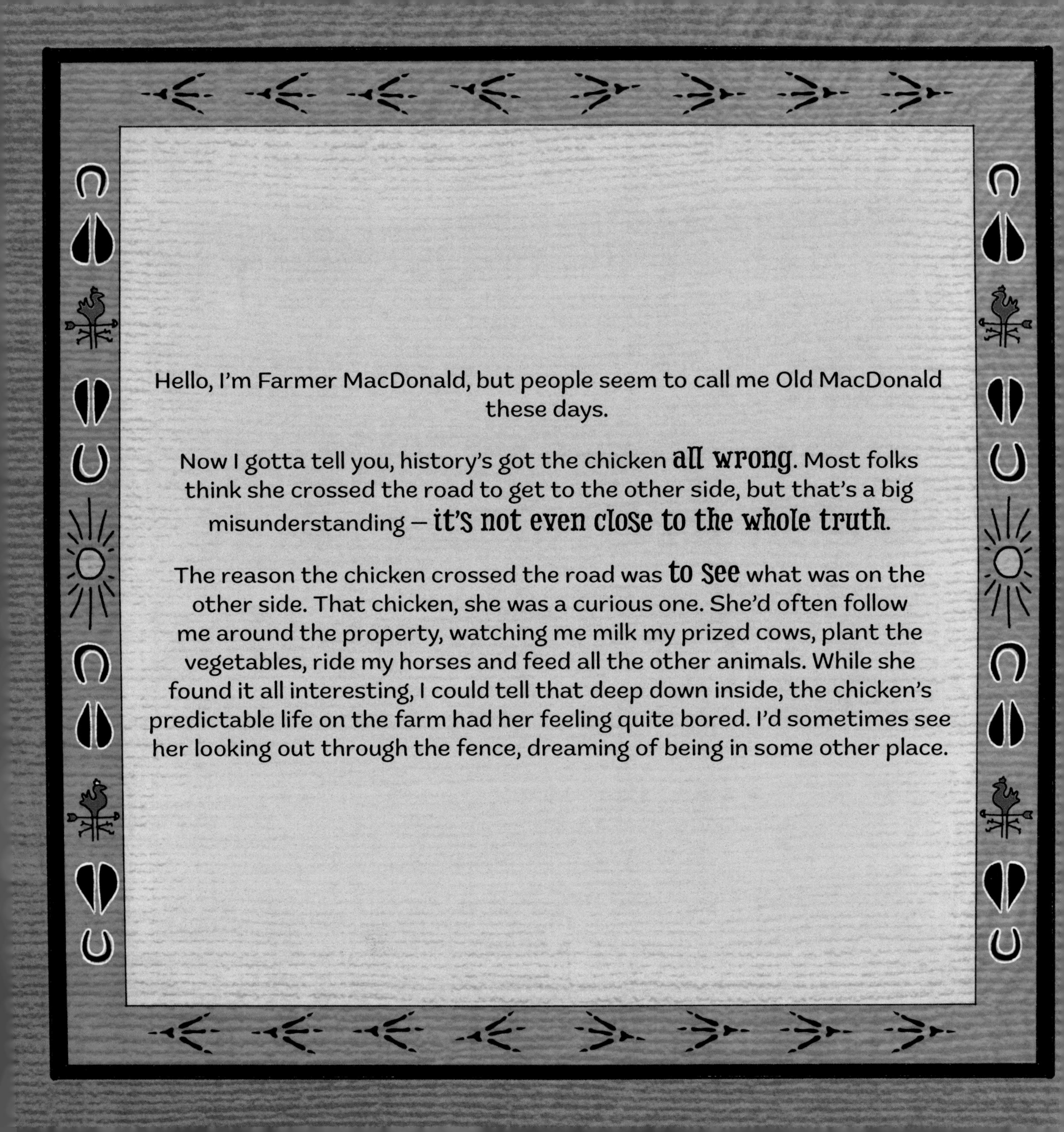

Hello, I'm Farmer MacDonald, but people seem to call me Old MacDonald these days.

Now I gotta tell you, history's got the chicken **all wrong**. Most folks think she crossed the road to get to the other side, but that's a big misunderstanding – **it's not even close to the whole truth.**

The reason the chicken crossed the road was **to see** what was on the other side. That chicken, she was a curious one. She'd often follow me around the property, watching me milk my prized cows, plant the vegetables, ride my horses and feed all the other animals. While she found it all interesting, I could tell that deep down inside, the chicken's predictable life on the farm had her feeling quite bored. I'd sometimes see her looking out through the fence, dreaming of being in some other place.

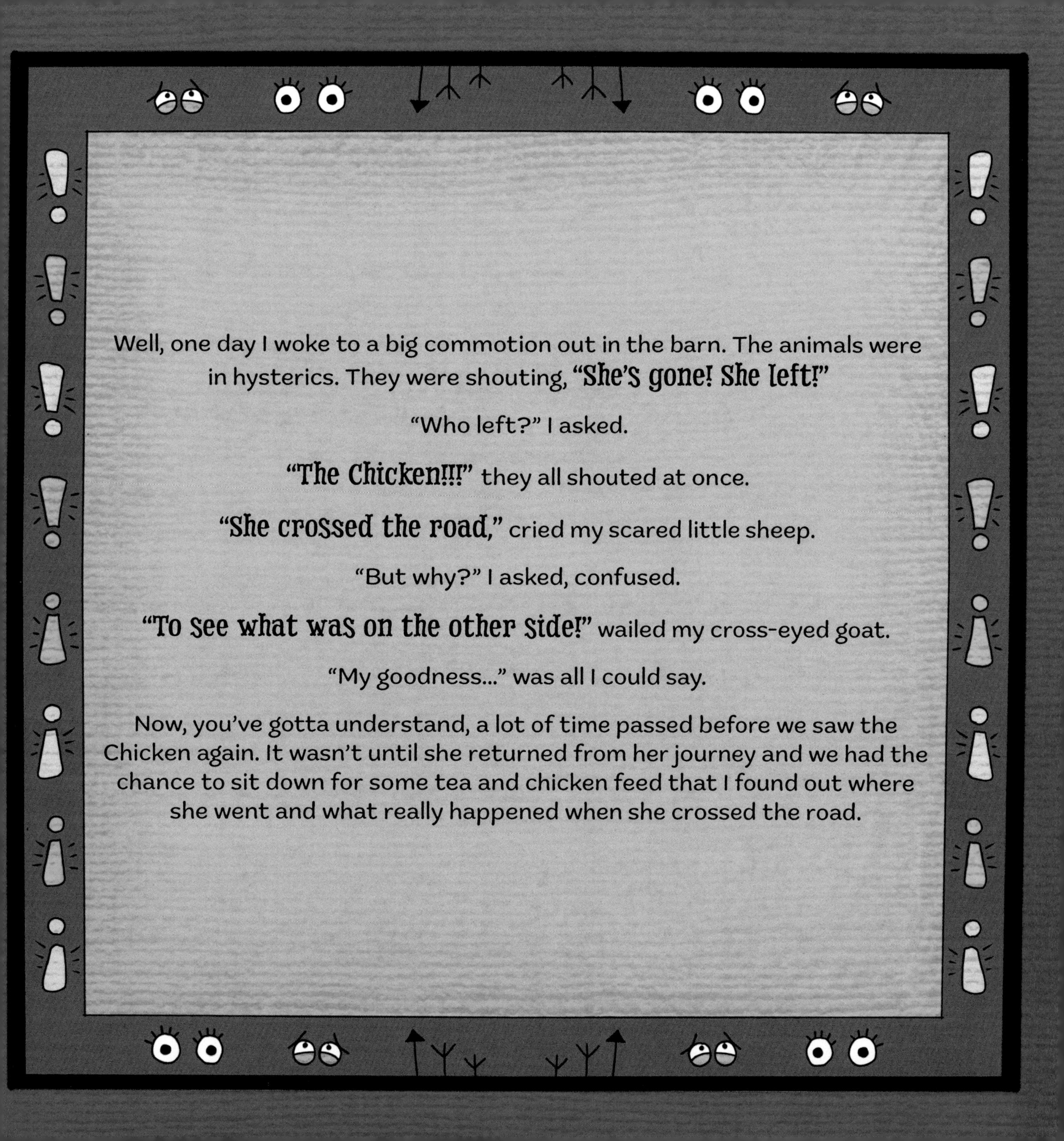

Well, one day I woke to a big commotion out in the barn. The animals were in hysterics. They were shouting, **"She's gone! She left!"**

"Who left?" I asked.

"The Chicken!!!" they all shouted at once.

"She crossed the road," cried my scared little sheep.

"But why?" I asked, confused.

"To see what was on the other side!" wailed my cross-eyed goat.

"My goodness..." was all I could say.

Now, you've gotta understand, a lot of time passed before we saw the Chicken again. It wasn't until she returned from her journey and we had the chance to sit down for some tea and chicken feed that I found out where she went and what really happened when she crossed the road.

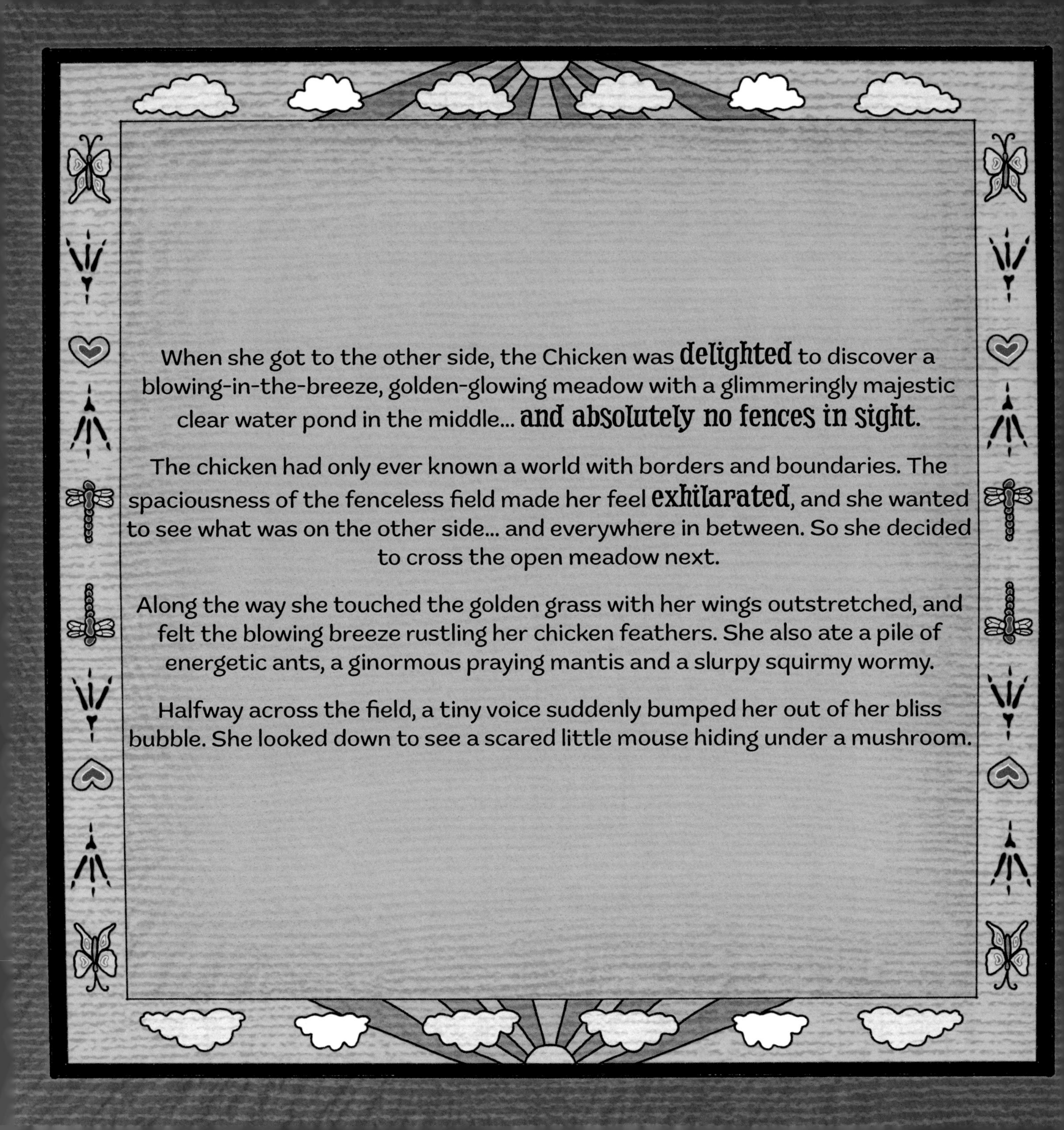

When she got to the other side, the Chicken was **delighted** to discover a blowing-in-the-breeze, golden-glowing meadow with a glimmeringly majestic clear water pond in the middle... **and absolutely no fences in sight.**

The chicken had only ever known a world with borders and boundaries. The spaciousness of the fenceless field made her feel **exhilarated**, and she wanted to see what was on the other side... and everywhere in between. So she decided to cross the open meadow next.

Along the way she touched the golden grass with her wings outstretched, and felt the blowing breeze rustling her chicken feathers. She also ate a pile of energetic ants, a ginormous praying mantis and a slurpy squirmy wormy.

Halfway across the field, a tiny voice suddenly bumped her out of her bliss bubble. She looked down to see a scared little mouse hiding under a mushroom.

"Get down Chicken! Get Down!" cried the mouse. Chicken was surprised to see such a scared little critter in such a splendid space.

"What's the matter mini mouse?" she inquired.

"It's a scary world out there Chicken. You better be careful and hide like me. There are bears, cougars, eagles and others that will want to **eat you!"** warned the mouse.

The names of these cool-sounding creatures made the chicken feel curious.

"Wow, I sure hope I'm lucky enough to meet one of them," she thought to herself, while not really paying much more attention to what the scaredy-mouse was saying.

"Thanks so much for the tip little mouse, but I can't spend my life hiding away. There's too much to live for, learn from and explore in this gigantically incredible world. I'll be sure to watch out for the creatures you mentioned. Who knows, maybe we'll even become friends!" she exclaimed hopefully, while continuing on her walk.

"Yah right. **Good luck with that Chicken!** Remember I warned you..." squeaked the mouse from the distance as the Chicken carried on, wondering if she would be lucky enough to meet one of these mystical-sounding creatures.

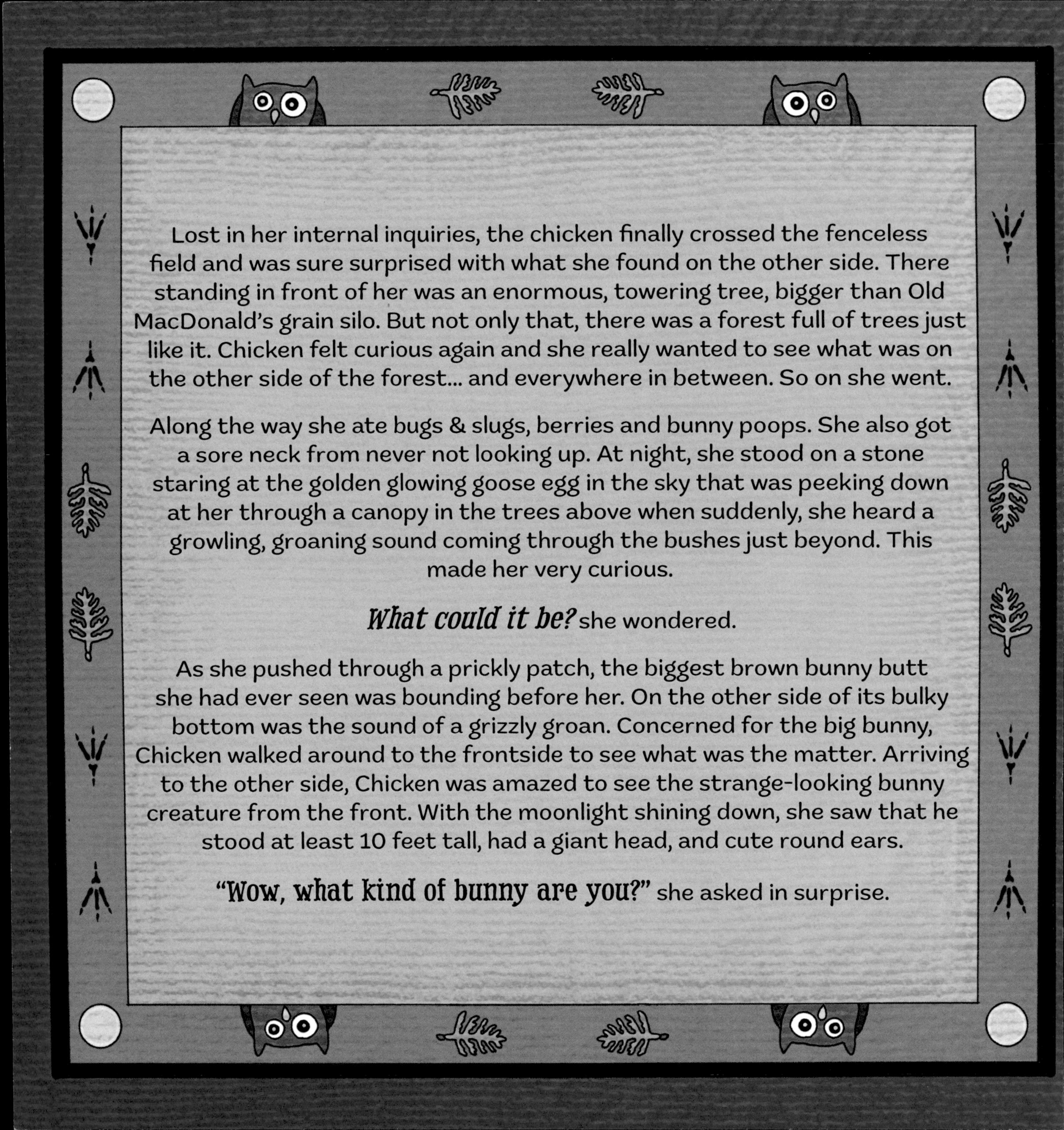

Lost in her internal inquiries, the chicken finally crossed the fenceless field and was sure surprised with what she found on the other side. There standing in front of her was an enormous, towering tree, bigger than Old MacDonald's grain silo. But not only that, there was a forest full of trees just like it. Chicken felt curious again and she really wanted to see what was on the other side of the forest... and everywhere in between. So on she went.

Along the way she ate bugs & slugs, berries and bunny poops. She also got a sore neck from never not looking up. At night, she stood on a stone staring at the golden glowing goose egg in the sky that was peeking down at her through a canopy in the trees above when suddenly, she heard a growling, groaning sound coming through the bushes just beyond. This made her very curious.

What could it be? she wondered.

As she pushed through a prickly patch, the biggest brown bunny butt she had ever seen was bounding before her. On the other side of its bulky bottom was the sound of a grizzly groan. Concerned for the big bunny, Chicken walked around to the frontside to see what was the matter. Arriving to the other side, Chicken was amazed to see the strange-looking bunny creature from the front. With the moonlight shining down, she saw that he stood at least 10 feet tall, had a giant head, and cute round ears.

"Wow, what kind of bunny are you?" she asked in surprise.

"Bunny? Ha! I'm a bear little chicken. Now leave me alone or I'll eat you for a midnight snack," answered the gruff Grizzly.

"Wow, you're a bear!? I've always wanted to meet one of you. My name's Chicken. What are you doing?" she curiously questioned while watching the bear jump up and down while groaning in discontent.

"I'm... trying... to... get... that... honey... hive" the bear replied between jumps, arms stretched upwards towards a hanging hive on a branch above.

"Oh, well maybe I can help!" exclaimed the chicken with excitement.

"Hah! You?" grumbled the bear, without taking his eyes off the prize.

"Yeah.... you... you..." Chicken stuttered as she thought fast. "You could stand on my back... or ummm... you could hang onto my back and I'll use my dinosaur feet to climb the tree... or wait, I've got it. I could grab you by the scruff of the neck and try to fly you up to the hive..." the chicken rambled at mach speed.

"Fly?" questioned the bear thoughtfully. "Fly!" he exclaimed as though he'd found a solution.

"I could throw you and you can use your wings to fly the rest of the way," he exclaimed.

Bear's idea made Chicken feel curious. Could she actually fly that high? She just had to find out. "Okay!" she enthusiastically declared. "Let's do it!"

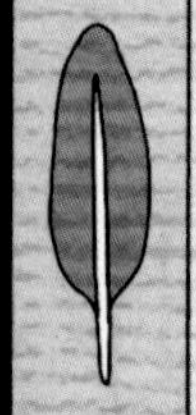 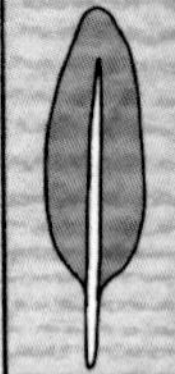

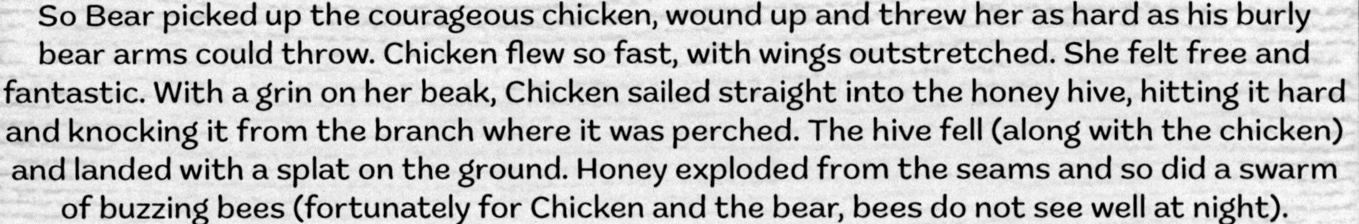

So Bear picked up the courageous chicken, wound up and threw her as hard as his burly bear arms could throw. Chicken flew so fast, with wings outstretched. She felt free and fantastic. With a grin on her beak, Chicken sailed straight into the honey hive, hitting it hard and knocking it from the branch where it was perched. The hive fell (along with the chicken) and landed with a splat on the ground. Honey exploded from the seams and so did a swarm of buzzing bees (fortunately for Chicken and the bear, bees do not see well at night).

"Nice Shot Chicken. Now come eat some honey!" yelled the bear in delight. The buzz of the sleepy, blurry eyed bees faded fast as they flew off into the darkness.

"Thanks!" said the grateful Grizzly between delicious honey slurps.

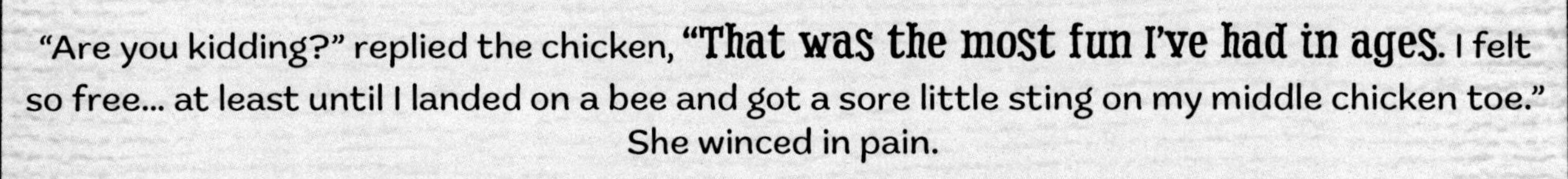

"Are you kidding?" replied the chicken, **"That was the most fun I've had in ages.** I felt so free... at least until I landed on a bee and got a sore little sting on my middle chicken toe." She winced in pain.

"Here Chicken, put a little honey on your toe to help heal the sting, and then chow down." Bear smeared a bit of honey on Chicken's swollen middle toe.

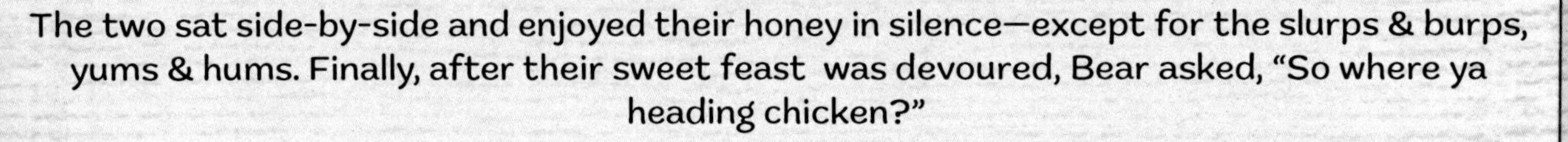

The two sat side-by-side and enjoyed their honey in silence—except for the slurps & burps, yums & hums. Finally, after their sweet feast was devoured, Bear asked, "So where ya heading chicken?"

"To the other side," the chicken replied with an affectionate smile.

"The other side of the forest?" Bear asked.

"Yeah, the forest," Chicken chimed cheerfully. "I want to see what's on the other side... and everywhere in between."

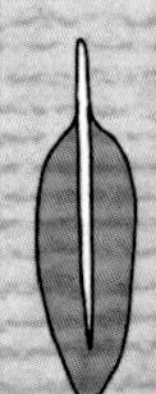

After a moment of contemplation, the bear said, "Well, I'm kind of heading in that direction and since you helped me, I'd like to help you too. So I'll take you along and you can ride on my head to rest your tingling toe."

Chicken agreed with a grin and jumped atop the bear's head.

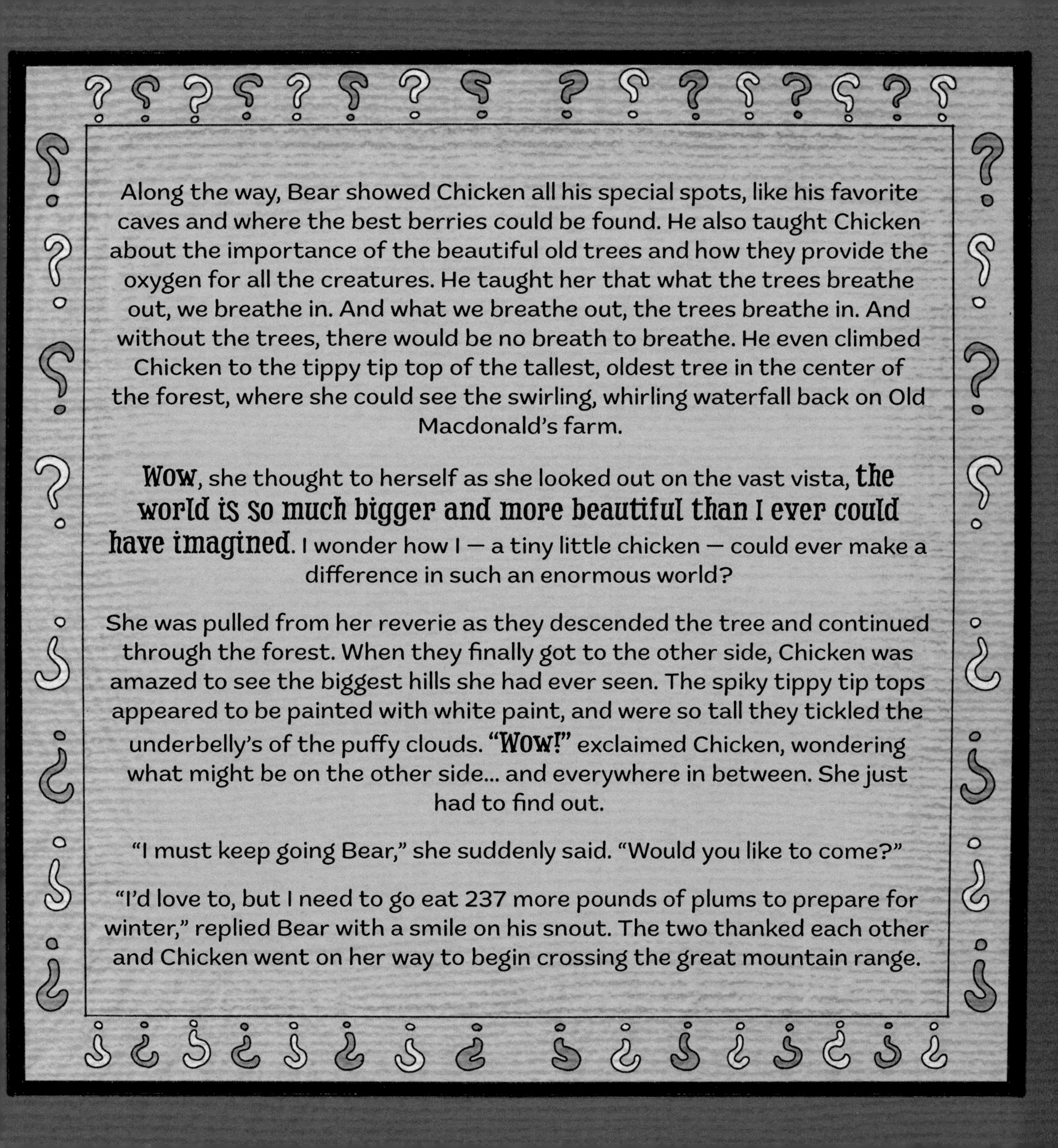

Along the way, Bear showed Chicken all his special spots, like his favorite caves and where the best berries could be found. He also taught Chicken about the importance of the beautiful old trees and how they provide the oxygen for all the creatures. He taught her that what the trees breathe out, we breathe in. And what we breathe out, the trees breathe in. And without the trees, there would be no breath to breathe. He even climbed Chicken to the tippy tip top of the tallest, oldest tree in the center of the forest, where she could see the swirling, whirling waterfall back on Old Macdonald's farm.

Wow, she thought to herself as she looked out on the vast vista, **the world is so much bigger and more beautiful than I ever could have imagined.** I wonder how I — a tiny little chicken — could ever make a difference in such an enormous world?

She was pulled from her reverie as they descended the tree and continued through the forest. When they finally got to the other side, Chicken was amazed to see the biggest hills she had ever seen. The spiky tippy tip tops appeared to be painted with white paint, and were so tall they tickled the underbelly's of the puffy clouds. **"Wow!"** exclaimed Chicken, wondering what might be on the other side... and everywhere in between. She just had to find out.

"I must keep going Bear," she suddenly said. "Would you like to come?"

"I'd love to, but I need to go eat 237 more pounds of plums to prepare for winter," replied Bear with a smile on his snout. The two thanked each other and Chicken went on her way to begin crossing the great mountain range.

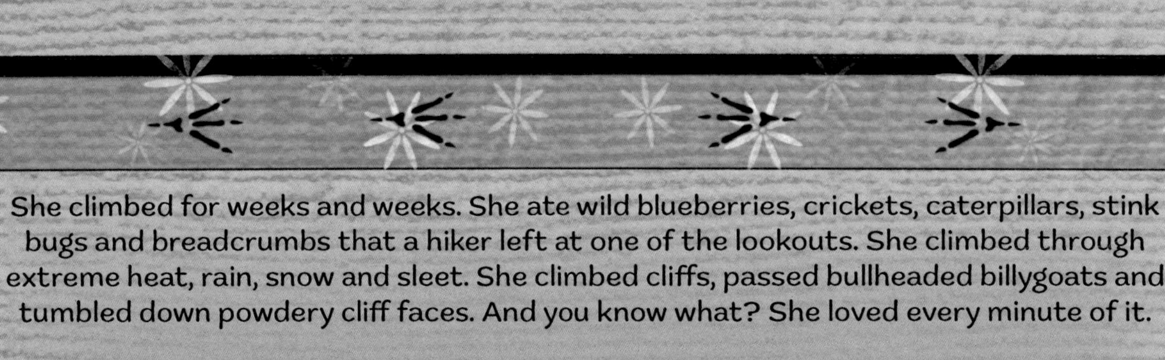

She climbed for weeks and weeks. She ate wild blueberries, crickets, caterpillars, stink bugs and breadcrumbs that a hiker left at one of the lookouts. She climbed through extreme heat, rain, snow and sleet. She climbed cliffs, passed bullheaded billygoats and tumbled down powdery cliff faces. And you know what? She loved every minute of it.

After several weeks of climbing, Chicken came across a crying cougar with a head-cold. Without knowing that this cougar was the very cat the little mouse in the meadow had warned her about, she naively approached the cuddly-looking colossal kitty cat with caring curiosity.

"What's wrong, big kitty?" the Chicken asked cordially as she approached the giant, 9-foot long, 150 pound pussy cat.

"I can't find my cubbies and with this cold, sniffing their scent is **impossible,"** she sobbed.

"Well, maybe I can help!" exclaimed the chicken with enthusiasm.

"But you're just a chicken, how could you possibly help me find my cubs?" the cougar mom moaned.

Ummm... well... Chicken thought quickly. "I could crow like a rooster to get their attention."

(she tried but nobody came).

"Or I could try flying up to that ledge to get a better view"

(she flapped her wings but just fluttered straight into the side of a rock).

"Oh, I know! I'll sniff them out with this beak of mine!" she exclaimed. "Droopy the hound dog back at the farm taught me to sniff out a needle in a haystack. What do your cubs smell like?" she asked.

"Ummm, like me," the cougar replied.

"Perfect!" clucked Chicken as she set off with her beak to the ground. The cougar chased behind sneezing and wheezing as Chicken sniffed high and low, hopping this way and that. Finally they came to a cave. Inside they found two cute little quivering cougar cubs.

"My cubbies!" cried the mama cougar as she leaped forward to rub foreheads with her babies. It was only then that the chicken noticed just how oddly enormous the cougar cat actually was.

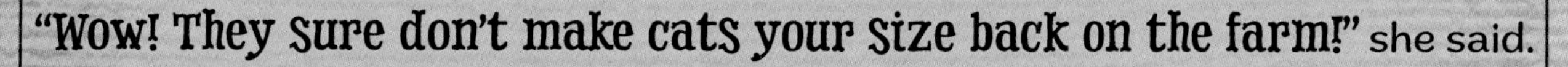

"Wow! They sure don't make cats your size back on the farm!" she said.

"That's because I'm a cougar," chuckled Mama Cougar.

"Woowwww, I've always wanted to meet one of you," Chicken exclaimed in awe.

"Well thank you for helping me reunite with my cubs little Chicken," purred Mama Cougar.

"You're welcome, big kitty cougar," said the Chicken. "It's really thanks to my furry friends back on the farm that I have such a well trained beak!"

"What are you doing up here so high in the mountains anyways?" questioned the cougar.

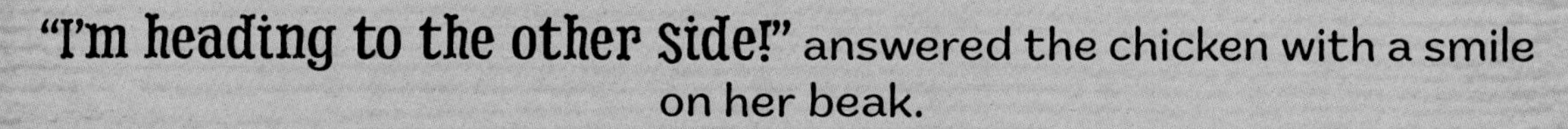

"I'm heading to the other side!" answered the chicken with a smile on her beak.

"Wow, that's ambitious!" said Mama Cougar. "I might be able to help you with that! Follow me cubs! And hop on my back little Chicken," she instructed. "I want to show you the other side!"

Away they went, running up ravines, climbing through caverns and stopping on a dime at the tippy tip top of the tallest powdery peak.

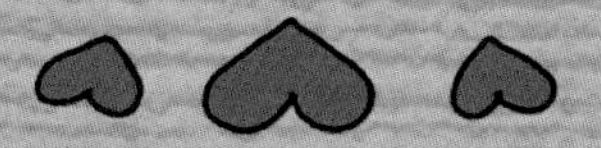

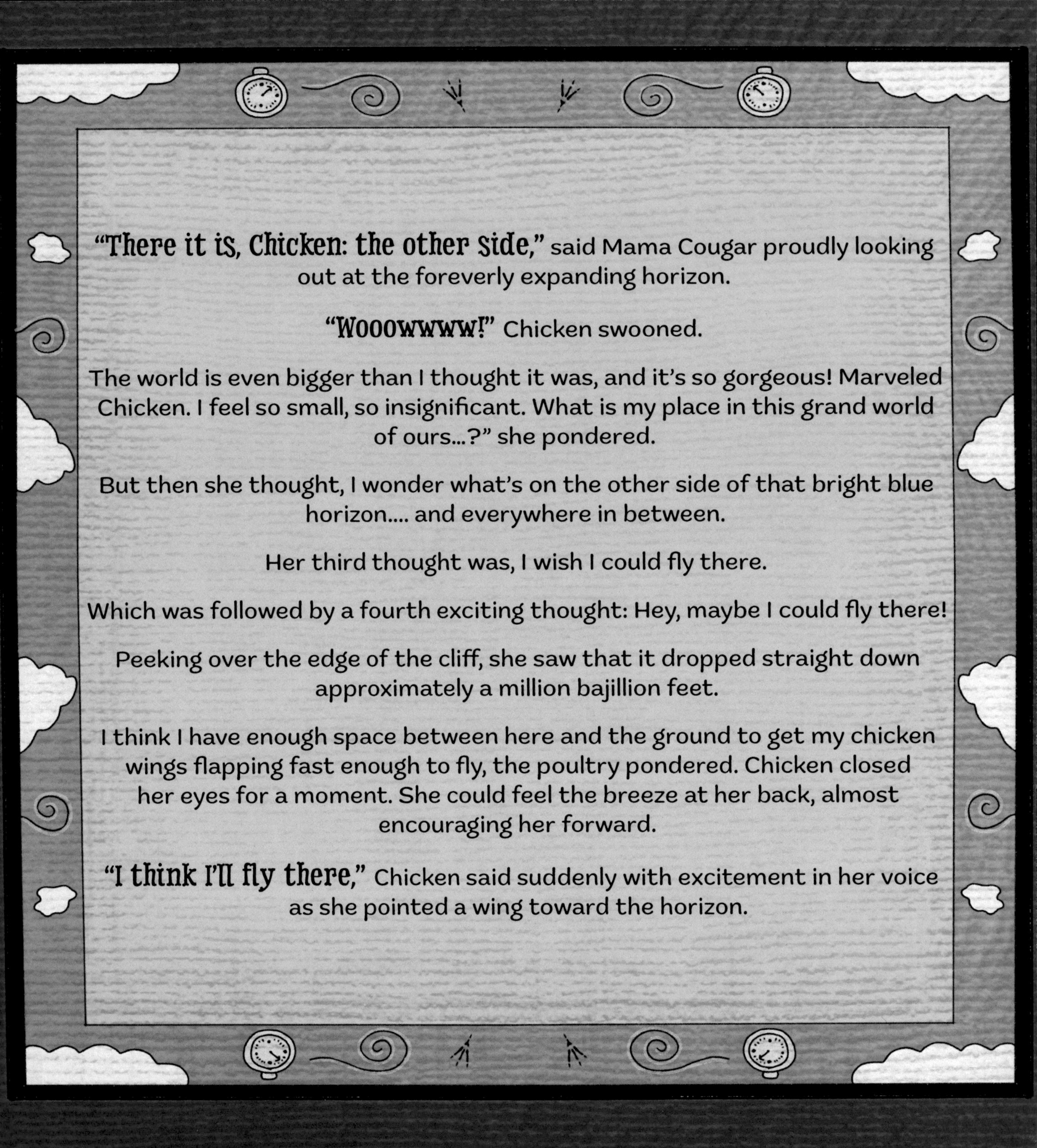

"There it is, Chicken: the other side," said Mama Cougar proudly looking out at the foreverly expanding horizon.

"Wooowwww!" Chicken swooned.

The world is even bigger than I thought it was, and it's so gorgeous! Marveled Chicken. I feel so small, so insignificant. What is my place in this grand world of ours...?" she pondered.

But then she thought, I wonder what's on the other side of that bright blue horizon.... and everywhere in between.

Her third thought was, I wish I could fly there.

Which was followed by a fourth exciting thought: Hey, maybe I could fly there!

Peeking over the edge of the cliff, she saw that it dropped straight down approximately a million bajillion feet.

I think I have enough space between here and the ground to get my chicken wings flapping fast enough to fly, the poultry pondered. Chicken closed her eyes for a moment. She could feel the breeze at her back, almost encouraging her forward.

"I think I'll fly there," Chicken said suddenly with excitement in her voice as she pointed a wing toward the horizon.

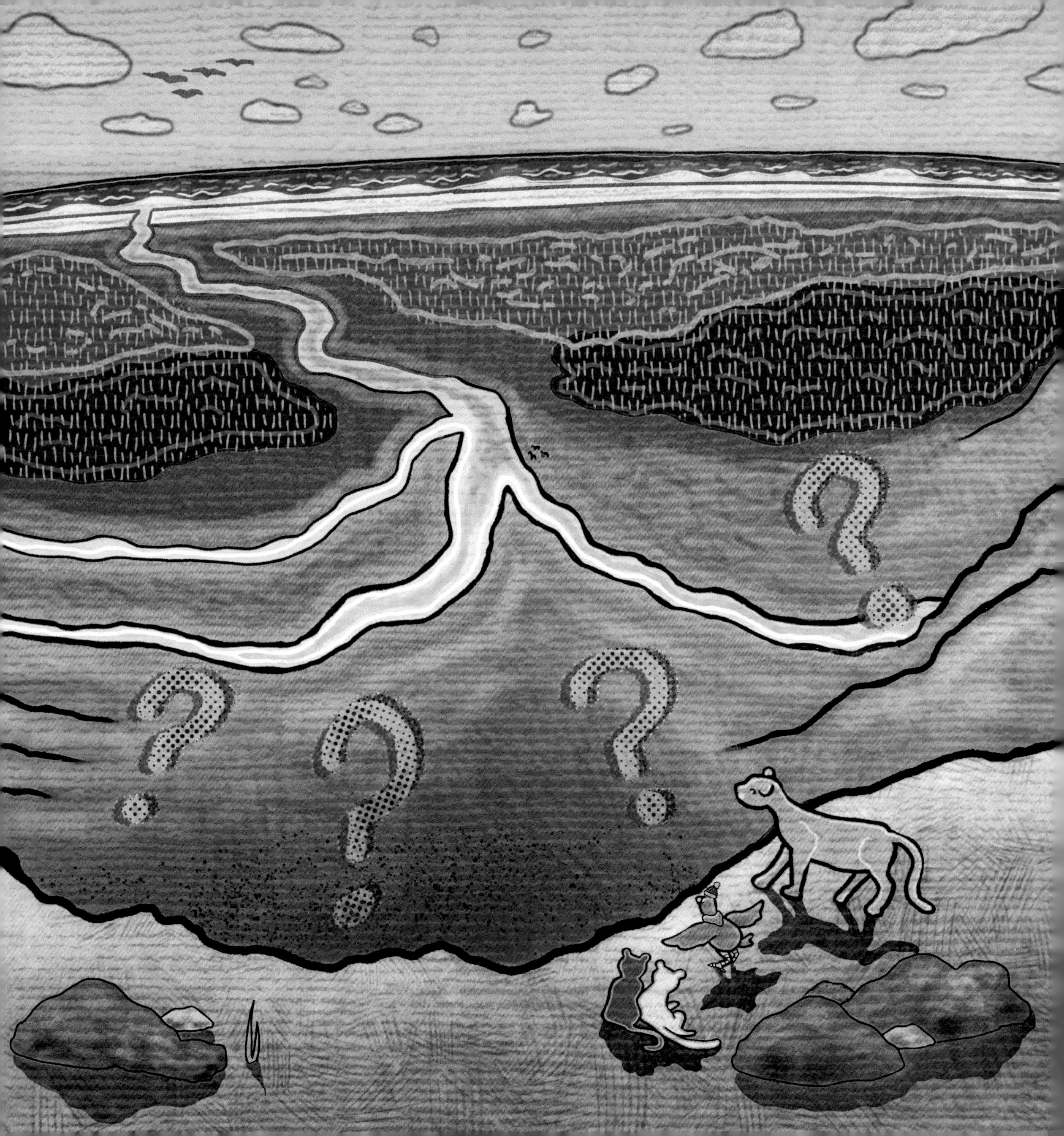

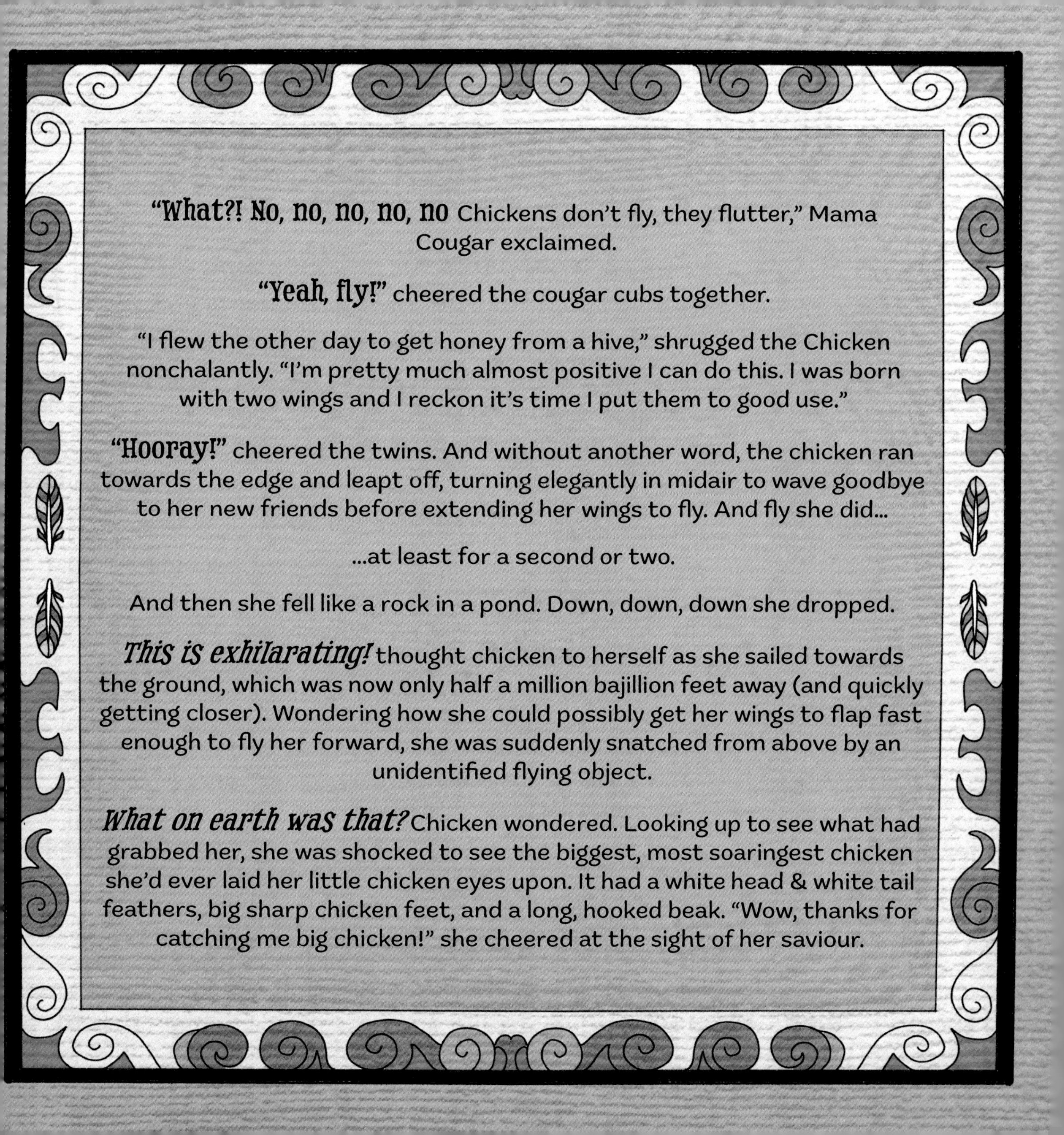

"**What?! No, no, no, no, no** Chickens don't fly, they flutter," Mama Cougar exclaimed.

"**Yeah, fly!**" cheered the cougar cubs together.

"I flew the other day to get honey from a hive," shrugged the Chicken nonchalantly. "I'm pretty much almost positive I can do this. I was born with two wings and I reckon it's time I put them to good use."

"**Hooray!**" cheered the twins. And without another word, the chicken ran towards the edge and leapt off, turning elegantly in midair to wave goodbye to her new friends before extending her wings to fly. And fly she did...

...at least for a second or two.

And then she fell like a rock in a pond. Down, down, down she dropped.

This is exhilarating! thought chicken to herself as she sailed towards the ground, which was now only half a million bajillion feet away (and quickly getting closer). Wondering how she could possibly get her wings to flap fast enough to fly her forward, she was suddenly snatched from above by an unidentified flying object.

What on earth was that? Chicken wondered. Looking up to see what had grabbed her, she was shocked to see the biggest, most soaringest chicken she'd ever laid her little chicken eyes upon. It had a white head & white tail feathers, big sharp chicken feet, and a long, hooked beak. "Wow, thanks for catching me big chicken!" she cheered at the sight of her saviour.

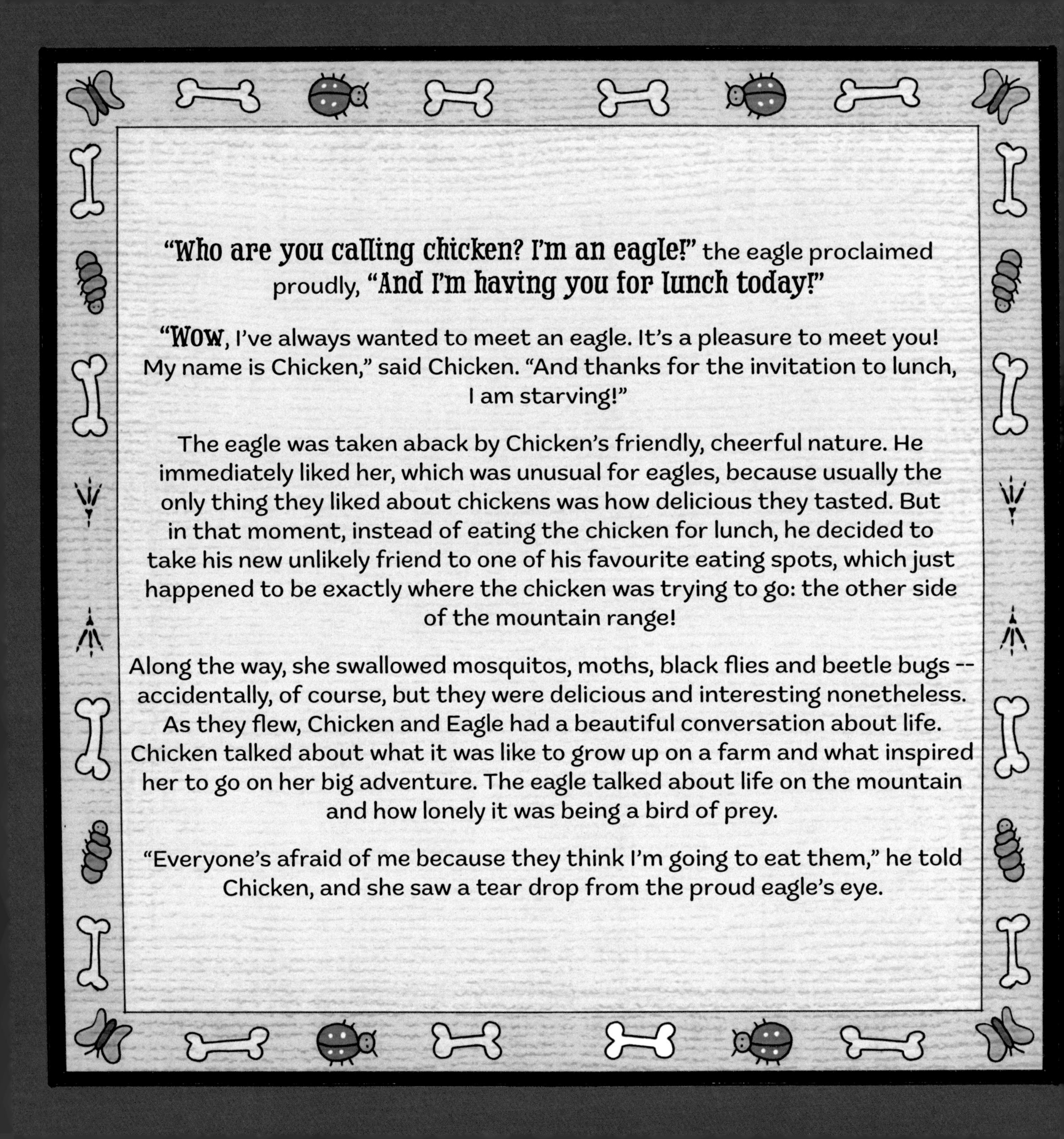

"Who are you calling chicken? I'm an eagle!" the eagle proclaimed proudly, **"And I'm having you for lunch today!"**

"**Wow**, I've always wanted to meet an eagle. It's a pleasure to meet you! My name is Chicken," said Chicken. "And thanks for the invitation to lunch, I am starving!"

The eagle was taken aback by Chicken's friendly, cheerful nature. He immediately liked her, which was unusual for eagles, because usually the only thing they liked about chickens was how delicious they tasted. But in that moment, instead of eating the chicken for lunch, he decided to take his new unlikely friend to one of his favourite eating spots, which just happened to be exactly where the chicken was trying to go: the other side of the mountain range!

Along the way, she swallowed mosquitos, moths, black flies and beetle bugs -- accidentally, of course, but they were delicious and interesting nonetheless. As they flew, Chicken and Eagle had a beautiful conversation about life. Chicken talked about what it was like to grow up on a farm and what inspired her to go on her big adventure. The eagle talked about life on the mountain and how lonely it was being a bird of prey.

"Everyone's afraid of me because they think I'm going to eat them," he told Chicken, and she saw a tear drop from the proud eagle's eye.

1 FLAP
2 FLAP
$F_D = \frac{1}{2} \rho v^2 C_d A$

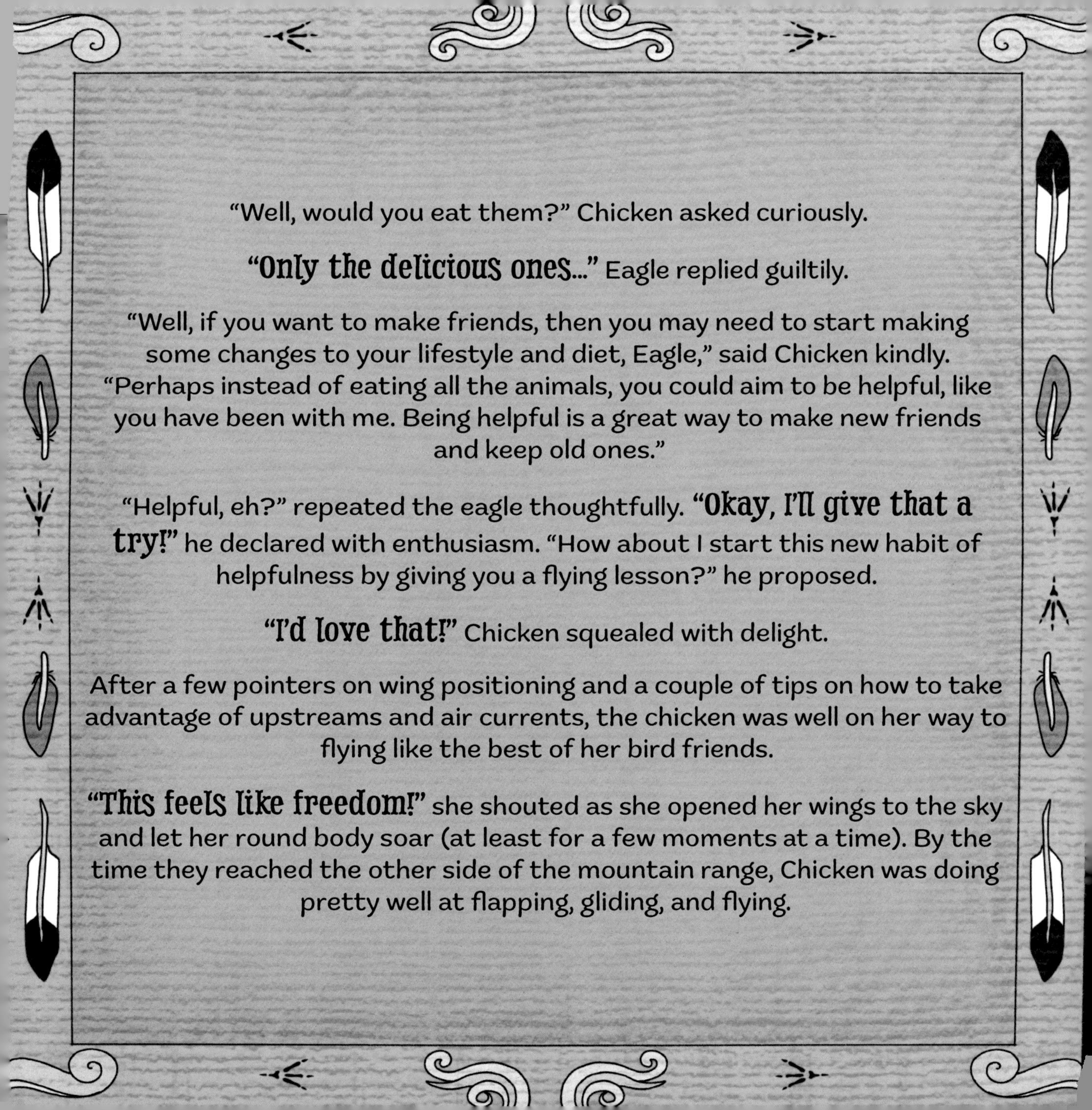

"Well, would you eat them?" Chicken asked curiously.

"Only the delicious ones..." Eagle replied guiltily.

"Well, if you want to make friends, then you may need to start making some changes to your lifestyle and diet, Eagle," said Chicken kindly. "Perhaps instead of eating all the animals, you could aim to be helpful, like you have been with me. Being helpful is a great way to make new friends and keep old ones."

"Helpful, eh?" repeated the eagle thoughtfully. **"Okay, I'll give that a try!"** he declared with enthusiasm. "How about I start this new habit of helpfulness by giving you a flying lesson?" he proposed.

"I'd love that!" Chicken squealed with delight.

After a few pointers on wing positioning and a couple of tips on how to take advantage of upstreams and air currents, the chicken was well on her way to flying like the best of her bird friends.

"This feels like freedom!" she shouted as she opened her wings to the sky and let her round body soar (at least for a few moments at a time). By the time they reached the other side of the mountain range, Chicken was doing pretty well at flapping, gliding, and flying.

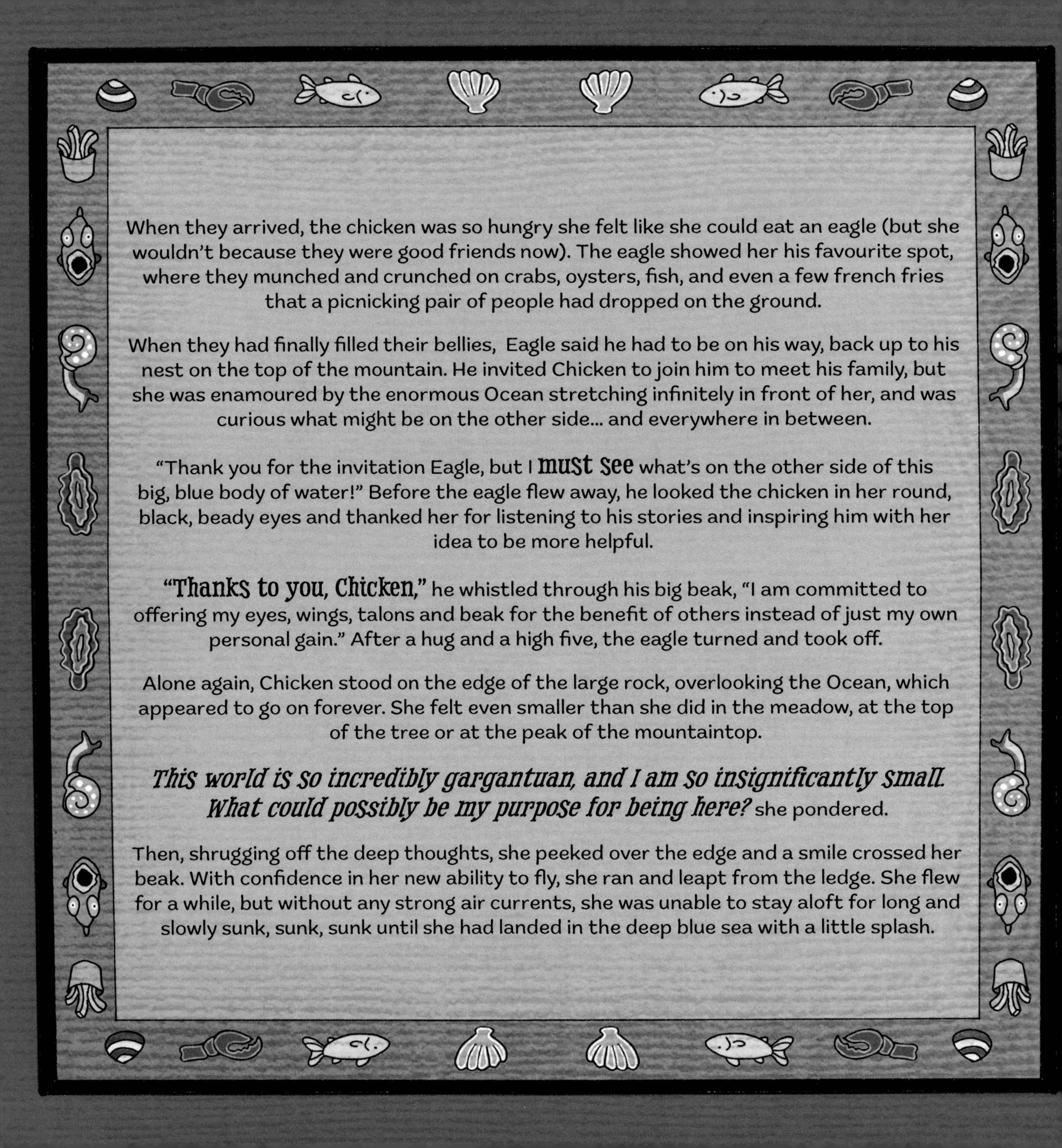

When they arrived, the chicken was so hungry she felt like she could eat an eagle (but she wouldn't because they were good friends now). The eagle showed her his favourite spot, where they munched and crunched on crabs, oysters, fish, and even a few french fries that a picnicking pair of people had dropped on the ground.

When they had finally filled their bellies, Eagle said he had to be on his way, back up to his nest on the top of the mountain. He invited Chicken to join him to meet his family, but she was enamoured by the enormous Ocean stretching infinitely in front of her, and was curious what might be on the other side... and everywhere in between.

"Thank you for the invitation Eagle, but I **must see** what's on the other side of this big, blue body of water!" Before the eagle flew away, he looked the chicken in her round, black, beady eyes and thanked her for listening to his stories and inspiring him with her idea to be more helpful.

"Thanks to you, Chicken," he whistled through his big beak, "I am committed to offering my eyes, wings, talons and beak for the benefit of others instead of just my own personal gain." After a hug and a high five, the eagle turned and took off.

Alone again, Chicken stood on the edge of the large rock, overlooking the Ocean, which appeared to go on forever. She felt even smaller than she did in the meadow, at the top of the tree or at the peak of the mountaintop.

This world is so incredibly gargantuan, and I am so insignificantly small. What could possibly be my purpose for being here? she pondered.

Then, shrugging off the deep thoughts, she peeked over the edge and a smile crossed her beak. With confidence in her new ability to fly, she ran and leapt from the ledge. She flew for a while, but without any strong air currents, she was unable to stay aloft for long and slowly sunk, sunk, sunk until she had landed in the deep blue sea with a little splash.

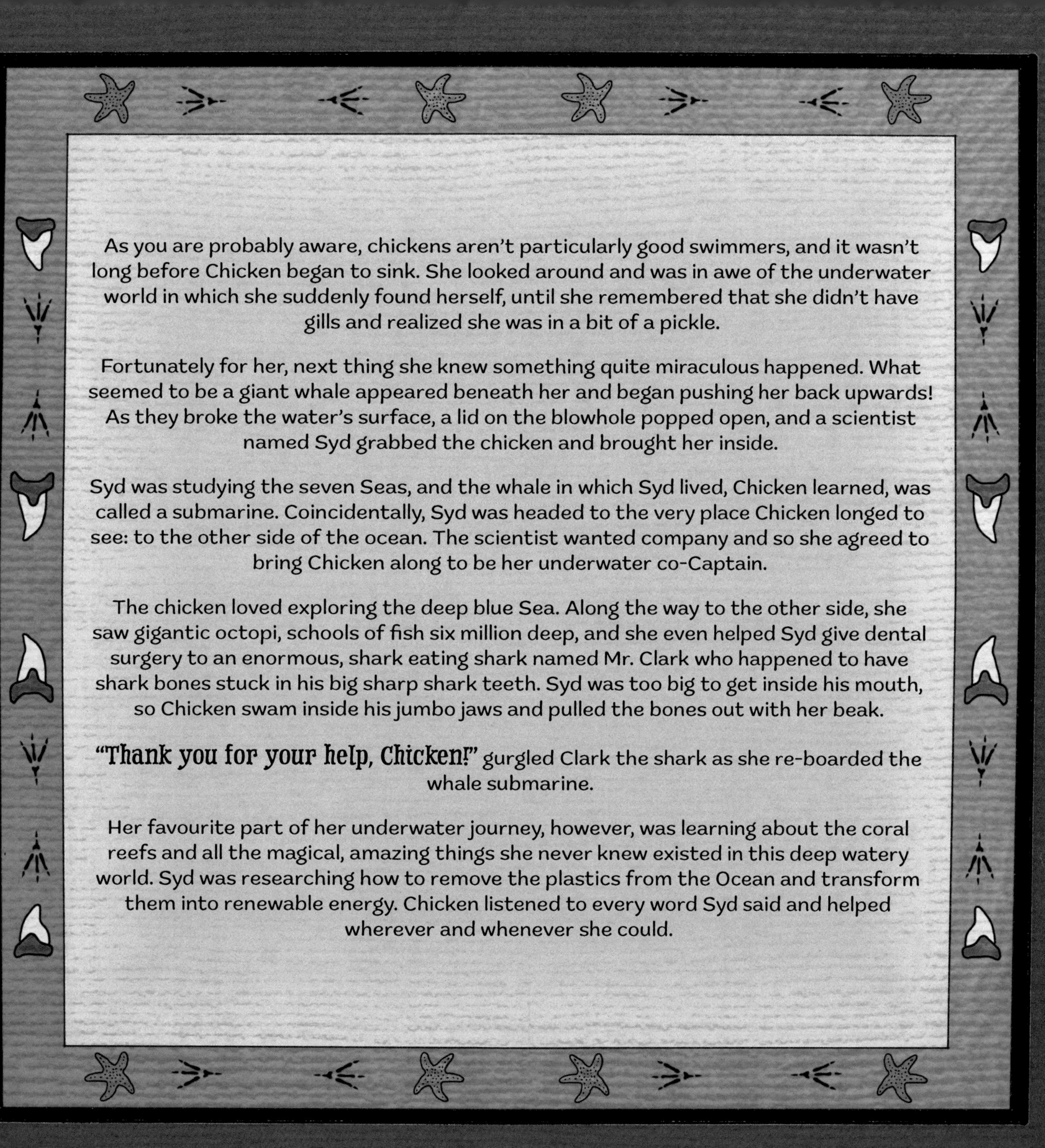

As you are probably aware, chickens aren't particularly good swimmers, and it wasn't long before Chicken began to sink. She looked around and was in awe of the underwater world in which she suddenly found herself, until she remembered that she didn't have gills and realized she was in a bit of a pickle.

Fortunately for her, next thing she knew something quite miraculous happened. What seemed to be a giant whale appeared beneath her and began pushing her back upwards! As they broke the water's surface, a lid on the blowhole popped open, and a scientist named Syd grabbed the chicken and brought her inside.

Syd was studying the seven Seas, and the whale in which Syd lived, Chicken learned, was called a submarine. Coincidentally, Syd was headed to the very place Chicken longed to see: to the other side of the ocean. The scientist wanted company and so she agreed to bring Chicken along to be her underwater co-Captain.

The chicken loved exploring the deep blue Sea. Along the way to the other side, she saw gigantic octopi, schools of fish six million deep, and she even helped Syd give dental surgery to an enormous, shark eating shark named Mr. Clark who happened to have shark bones stuck in his big sharp shark teeth. Syd was too big to get inside his mouth, so Chicken swam inside his jumbo jaws and pulled the bones out with her beak.

"Thank you for your help, Chicken!" gurgled Clark the shark as she re-boarded the whale submarine.

Her favourite part of her underwater journey, however, was learning about the coral reefs and all the magical, amazing things she never knew existed in this deep watery world. Syd was researching how to remove the plastics from the Ocean and transform them into renewable energy. Chicken listened to every word Syd said and helped wherever and whenever she could.

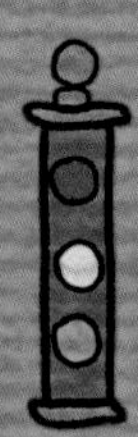
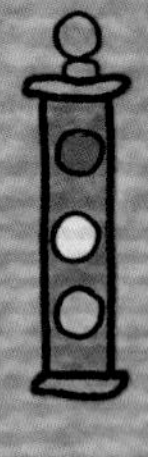

Finally, they reached the other side of the Ocean and rose to the surface once again. When the hatch of the sub popped open and Chicken stuck her little head out, a giant crowd of people were standing there cheering for her. The chicken made headlines across the world for being the first deep sea poultry to cross the ocean submerged in a submarine. But the chicken was too enthralled with the gigantic mega city that lay before her to care much about the praise. The buildings tickled the tummies of the clouds in the sky, and the winding streets wound on forever.

My goodness, I feel so teensy tiny in this immensely massive world, Chicken pondered yet again, as she realized the world was yet again even bigger than she could ever have imagined!

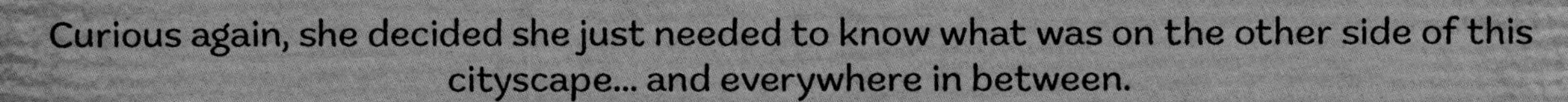

Curious again, she decided she just needed to know what was on the other side of this cityscape... and everywhere in between.

So with a wave of her wing, she said, "So long!" to Syd and off she went to see what there was to discover. "Goode-Bye Chicken. Thank you for your help and good company. I will miss you!"" Syd called after her as Chicken squeezed past her adoring fans.

Chicken walked the streets until her tired legs were tuckered out, at which point she stuck out a wing and hitched a ride with a scooter driver named Clide. Clide was a happy chap, and spent his days zigging, zagging and zipping around the city, driving people wherever
they wanted to go. Chicken was itching to see every inch of this urban jungle, as well as what was on the other side of it. Clide happily obliged and showed her all his favourite sights in the city.

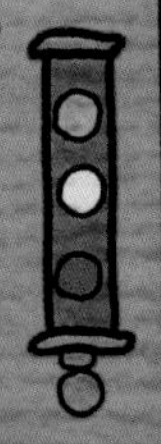

"Over here is the tallest building in the world!"

"This is the largest dinosaur exhibit in the world!"

"This is my favourite place to eat unpickled pickles in the world!"

144
EXPLORING CHICKEN VISITS TOWN!
METRO NEWS

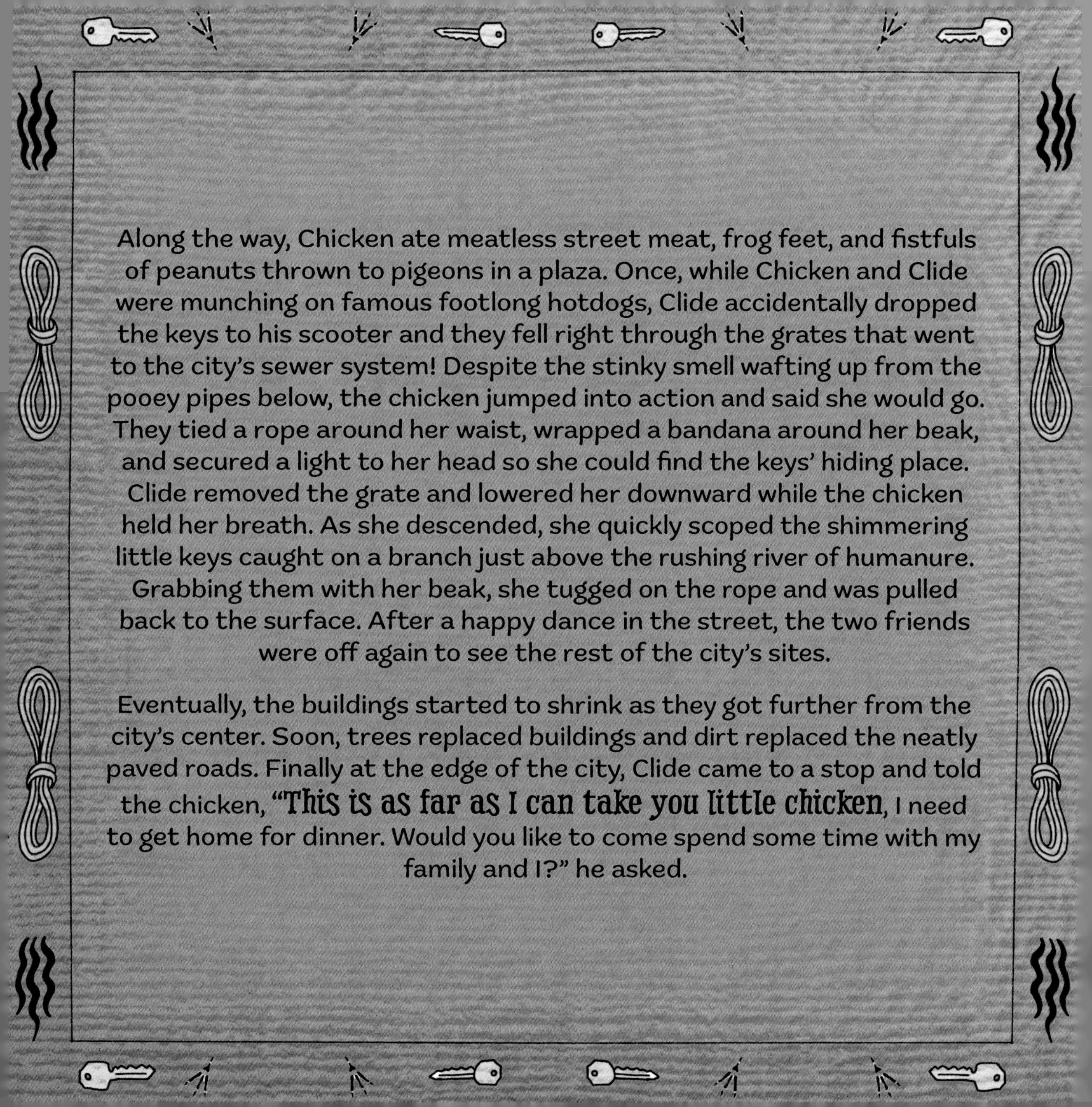

Along the way, Chicken ate meatless street meat, frog feet, and fistfuls of peanuts thrown to pigeons in a plaza. Once, while Chicken and Clide were munching on famous footlong hotdogs, Clide accidentally dropped the keys to his scooter and they fell right through the grates that went to the city's sewer system! Despite the stinky smell wafting up from the pooey pipes below, the chicken jumped into action and said she would go. They tied a rope around her waist, wrapped a bandana around her beak, and secured a light to her head so she could find the keys' hiding place. Clide removed the grate and lowered her downward while the chicken held her breath. As she descended, she quickly scoped the shimmering little keys caught on a branch just above the rushing river of humanure. Grabbing them with her beak, she tugged on the rope and was pulled back to the surface. After a happy dance in the street, the two friends were off again to see the rest of the city's sites.

Eventually, the buildings started to shrink as they got further from the city's center. Soon, trees replaced buildings and dirt replaced the neatly paved roads. Finally at the edge of the city, Clide came to a stop and told the chicken, "This is as far as I can take you little chicken, I need to get home for dinner. Would you like to come spend some time with my family and I?" he asked.

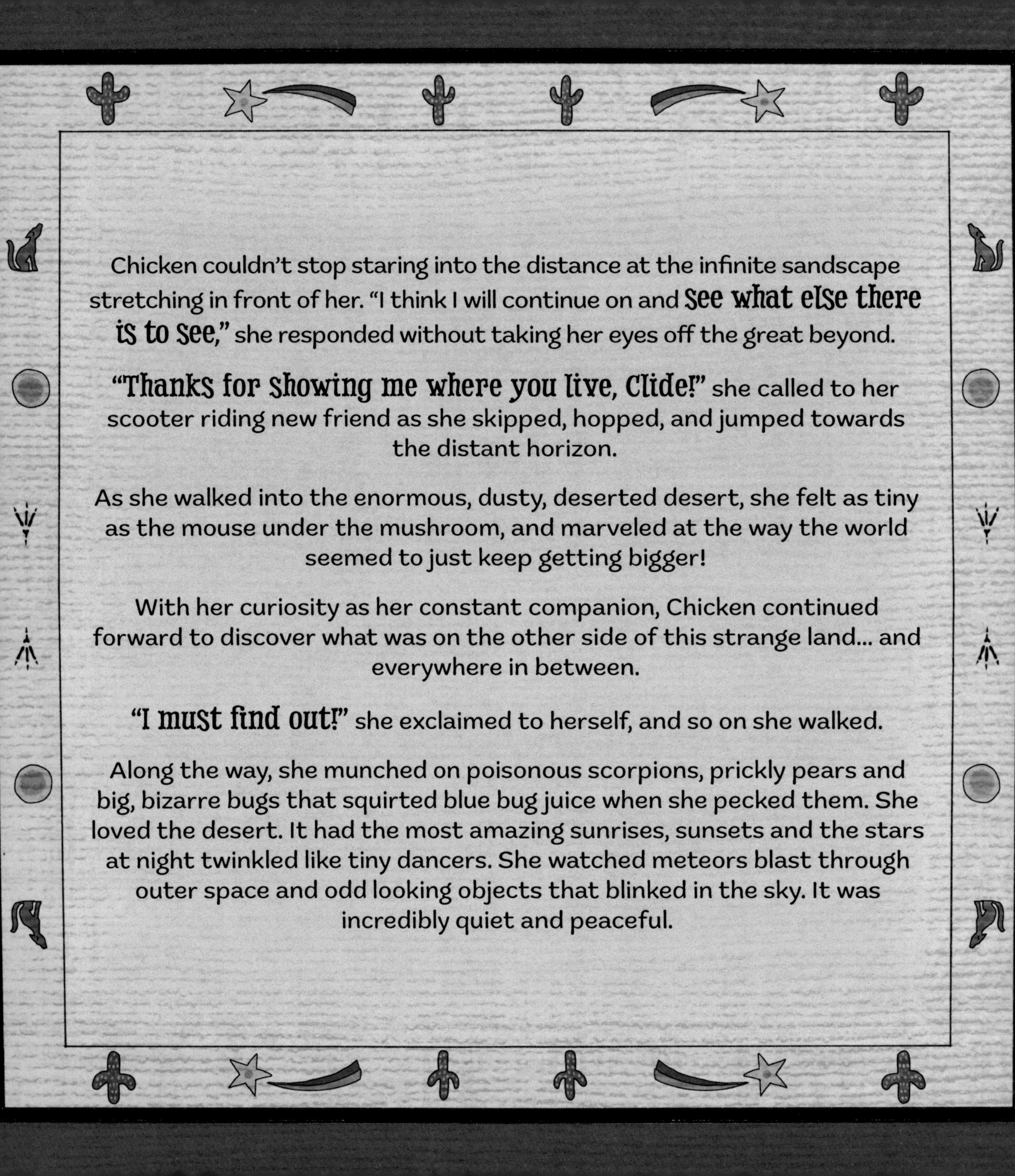

Chicken couldn't stop staring into the distance at the infinite sandscape stretching in front of her. "I think I will continue on and **see what else there is to see,"** she responded without taking her eyes off the great beyond.

"Thanks for showing me where you live, Clide!" she called to her scooter riding new friend as she skipped, hopped, and jumped towards the distant horizon.

As she walked into the enormous, dusty, deserted desert, she felt as tiny as the mouse under the mushroom, and marveled at the way the world seemed to just keep getting bigger!

With her curiosity as her constant companion, Chicken continued forward to discover what was on the other side of this strange land... and everywhere in between.

"I must find out!" she exclaimed to herself, and so on she walked.

Along the way, she munched on poisonous scorpions, prickly pears and big, bizarre bugs that squirted blue bug juice when she pecked them. She loved the desert. It had the most amazing sunrises, sunsets and the stars at night twinkled like tiny dancers. She watched meteors blast through outer space and odd looking objects that blinked in the sky. It was incredibly quiet and peaceful.

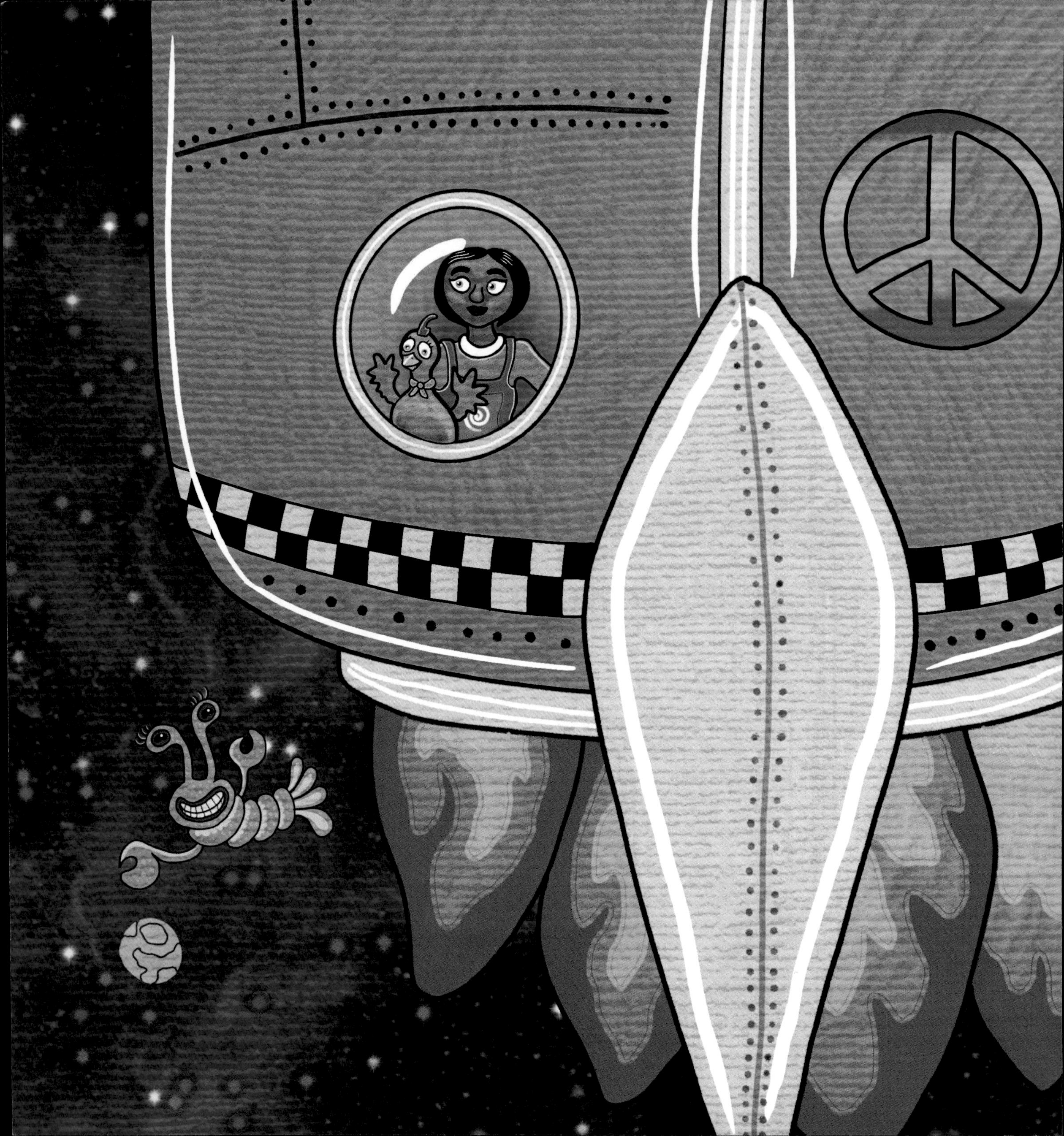

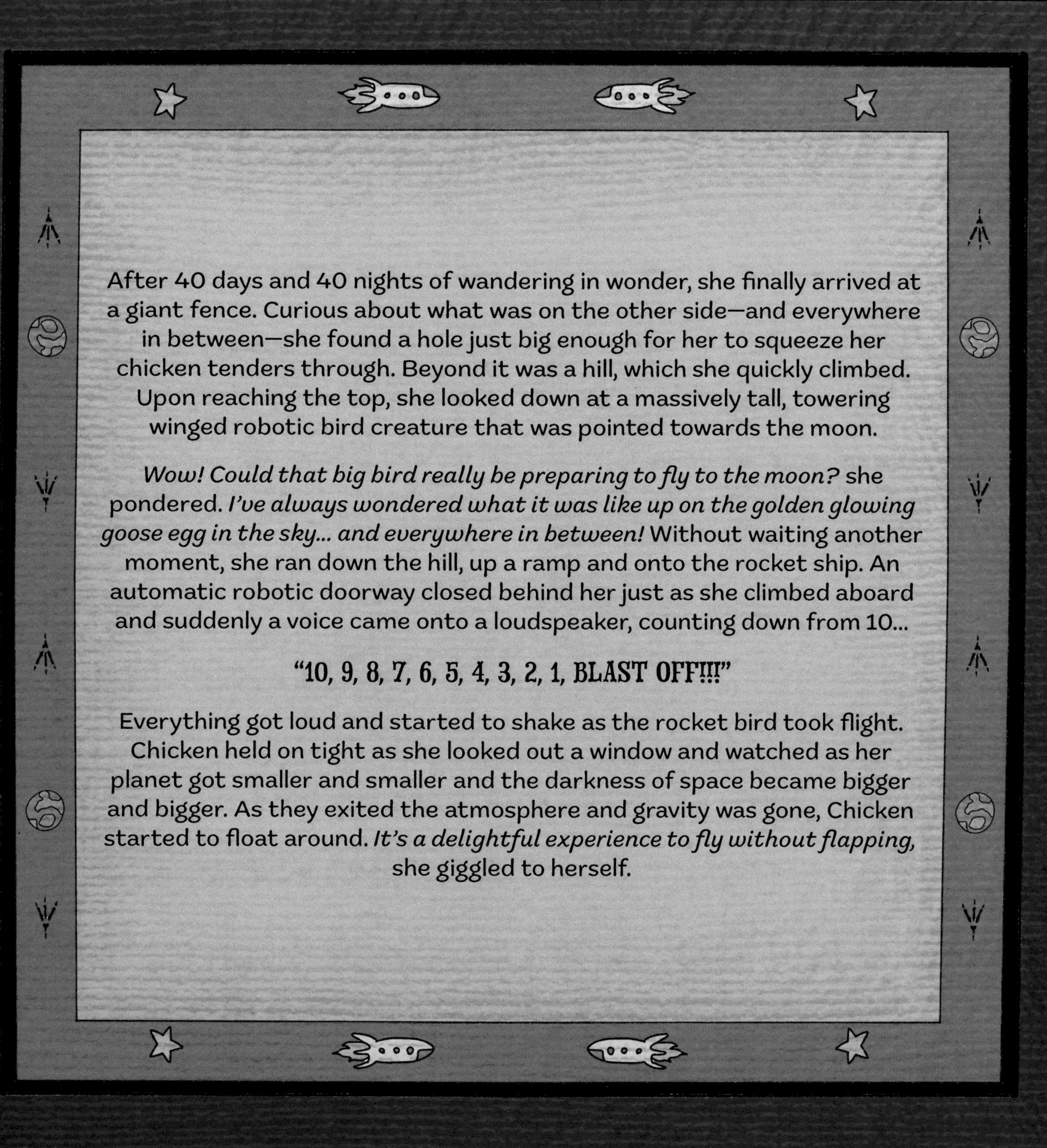

After 40 days and 40 nights of wandering in wonder, she finally arrived at a giant fence. Curious about what was on the other side—and everywhere in between—she found a hole just big enough for her to squeeze her chicken tenders through. Beyond it was a hill, which she quickly climbed. Upon reaching the top, she looked down at a massively tall, towering winged robotic bird creature that was pointed towards the moon.

Wow! Could that big bird really be preparing to fly to the moon? she pondered. *I've always wondered what it was like up on the golden glowing goose egg in the sky... and everywhere in between!* Without waiting another moment, she ran down the hill, up a ramp and onto the rocket ship. An automatic robotic doorway closed behind her just as she climbed aboard and suddenly a voice came onto a loudspeaker, counting down from 10...

"10, 9, 8, 7, 6, 5, 4, 3, 2, 1, BLAST OFF!!!"

Everything got loud and started to shake as the rocket bird took flight. Chicken held on tight as she looked out a window and watched as her planet got smaller and smaller and the darkness of space became bigger and bigger. As they exited the atmosphere and gravity was gone, Chicken started to float around. *It's a delightful experience to fly without flapping,* she giggled to herself.

Curious to explore and see more, she floated down a hallway and into the nose of the bird-ship where she met an astronaut named Amethyst (who liked being called Amy). Amy was excited to meet her new space friend, and relieved that she'd have company on her solo mission to the moon.

The two got along great, like two rocket-peas in a space-pod, and Chicken got to eat all sorts of interesting foods like capsuled carrots, liquid legumes and powdered pears. She also helped Amy push buttons, pull levers, fold space laundry and do routine checks of all their high-tech doohickies (which is the official technical term for "space gadgets.")

Finally, they made a safe landing on the dark side of the moon where they were to get out and collect space rocks. Unfortunately for Amy, when she pulled her space-suit from her closet, she discovered that Chicken wasn't the only creature who'd hopped on board! A hungry moth had joined the flight as well, and had munched a behemoth-sized hole in Amy's spacesuit, making it impossible for Amy to leave the ship. Luckily, Amy had an extra astronaut suit that fit Chicken perfectly. **"Would you be willing to go onto the moon and collect our moon rock samples?"** Amy asked hopefully.

"Absotuciously!" cried the chicken, wondering what it would be like to walk on the moon.

Well, truth be told, Chicken was the first poultry ever on the moon. She loved the feeling of weightlessness as she bounced over craters and bounded over moon rocks.

BURP!

After collecting the samples, Chicken stood in the deep lunar stillness for a moment and stared back at the earth. Her home planet, which had once felt incomprehensibly large, now looked insignificantly - almost pathetically- small compared to the vastness of infinite space that surrounded it. The majestic enormity of it took her breath away, and at once made her feel littler than small, smaller than incy wincy, incy wincier than itty bitty, and itty bittier than infinitesimally tiny.

"In a universe so vast, so enormous, so expansively, unfathomably, inexhaustibly, gargantiously, ginormous, how could a life as small as mine even matter? What is it all for? **What could be my purpose amongst such magnitude and magnificence?"** Chicken questioned out loud to herself.

Not realizing her walkie-talkie radio was on, she was surprised to hear the sound of Amy's voice in her ear, answering her inspiring inquiry.

"My sweet, cheerful chicken friend--**YOU** are the purpose in all of this infinite expansiveness. It is your joy and delight for discovering worlds unseen, your energetic, insatiable curiosity that pulls you towards the unknown, your happy, helpful nature that touches the hearts of those you encounter - it is these beautiful, extraordinary, and unique qualities that make your life matter. Each time you inspire others or make them feel heard, seen, or supported, you are letting life live through you, and by letting life live through you, you let life thrive. By connecting to the ever present magic and serendipity that surrounds you, you keep the magic of life alive.

You may feel small, dear Chicken, but within your little beating chicken heart, you contain the infinite vastness of space. What you see out there is simply your own reflection, smiling back at you. **You are part of all of it, and all of it is part of you."**

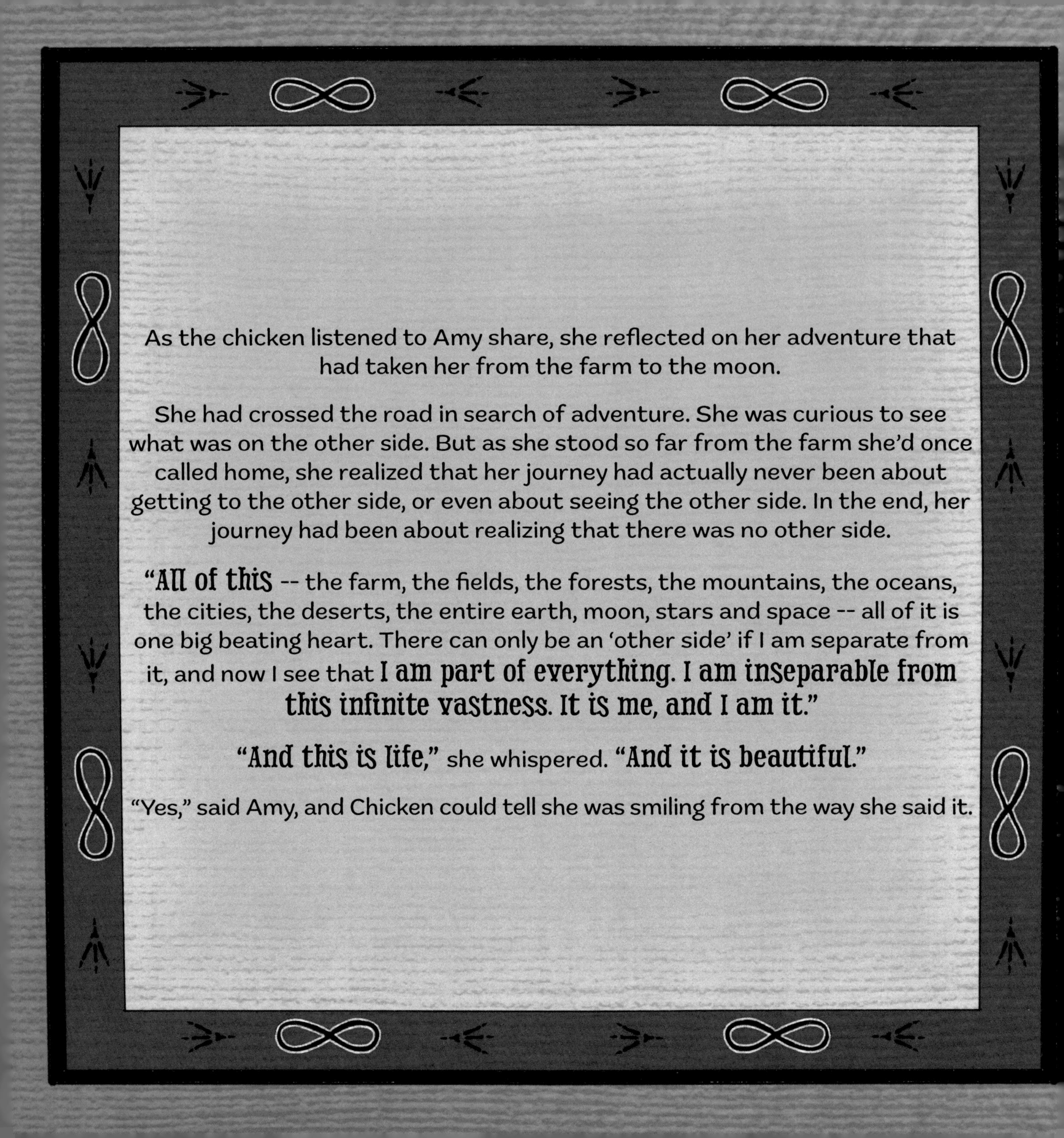

As the chicken listened to Amy share, she reflected on her adventure that had taken her from the farm to the moon.

She had crossed the road in search of adventure. She was curious to see what was on the other side. But as she stood so far from the farm she'd once called home, she realized that her journey had actually never been about getting to the other side, or even about seeing the other side. In the end, her journey had been about realizing that there was no other side.

"**All of this** -- the farm, the fields, the forests, the mountains, the oceans, the cities, the deserts, the entire earth, moon, stars and space -- all of it is one big beating heart. There can only be an 'other side' if I am separate from it, and now I see that **I am part of everything. I am inseparable from this infinite vastness. It is me, and I am it.**"

"**And this is life,**" she whispered. "**And it is beautiful.**"

"Yes," said Amy, and Chicken could tell she was smiling from the way she said it.

POULTRY POWER
WELCOME BACK CHICKEN!

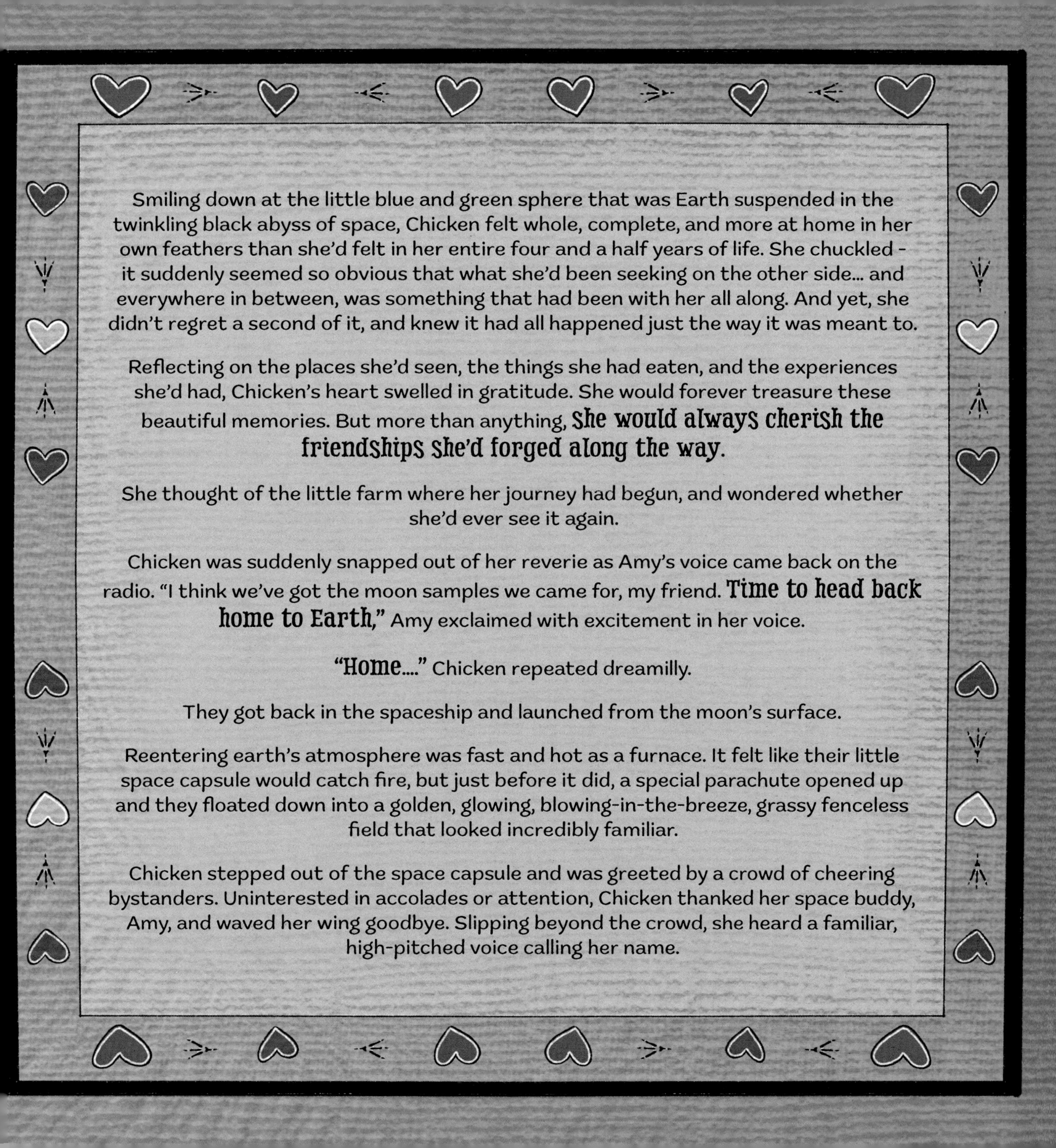

Smiling down at the little blue and green sphere that was Earth suspended in the twinkling black abyss of space, Chicken felt whole, complete, and more at home in her own feathers than she'd felt in her entire four and a half years of life. She chuckled - it suddenly seemed so obvious that what she'd been seeking on the other side... and everywhere in between, was something that had been with her all along. And yet, she didn't regret a second of it, and knew it had all happened just the way it was meant to.

Reflecting on the places she'd seen, the things she had eaten, and the experiences she'd had, Chicken's heart swelled in gratitude. She would forever treasure these beautiful memories. But more than anything, **she would always cherish the friendships she'd forged along the way.**

She thought of the little farm where her journey had begun, and wondered whether she'd ever see it again.

Chicken was suddenly snapped out of her reverie as Amy's voice came back on the radio. "I think we've got the moon samples we came for, my friend. **Time to head back home to Earth,"** Amy exclaimed with excitement in her voice.

"Home...." Chicken repeated dreamilly.

They got back in the spaceship and launched from the moon's surface.

Reentering earth's atmosphere was fast and hot as a furnace. It felt like their little space capsule would catch fire, but just before it did, a special parachute opened up and they floated down into a golden, glowing, blowing-in-the-breeze, grassy fenceless field that looked incredibly familiar.

Chicken stepped out of the space capsule and was greeted by a crowd of cheering bystanders. Uninterested in accolades or attention, Chicken thanked her space buddy, Amy, and waved her wing goodbye. Slipping beyond the crowd, she heard a familiar, high-pitched voice calling her name.

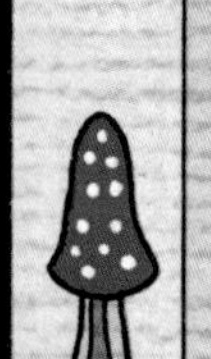

"Chicken! Chicken! You're still alive?!" squeaked the scared little mouse from under their mushroom.

"Hi Mouse!" Chicken squealed in delight to see a familiar friend.

"Where have you been?" asked the mouse.

"You will not believe how magnificent this world is," answered Chicken. "I made friends with a big burly bear, a couple of cougar cubs, an enormous eagle bird, a shark eating shark named Mr. Clark, a scooter driver named Clide, a scientist named Syd and I even went to the moon and back again with my astronaut friend Amy...." the chicken trailed off gazing towards a paved road just beyond a clear water pond.

The mouse was perplexed, unsure if the chicken was pulling his leg with her far-fetched story. But he didn't have time to question her tall tale because Chicken started to walk toward the road ahead, which looked strangely familiar. Along the way she felt the golden grass with her wings outstretched while the blowing breeze rustled her chicken feathers.

"You're a wild one Chicken, but I like you!" squeaked the curious little mouse from behind her. "I think maybe I'll try seeing the world someday too."

The chicken arrived at the edge of the paved road and took a look back towards the towering forest on the other side, with the monumental mountains beyond that and an expansive ocean, skyscraping cities, dusty deserts and more beyond those...

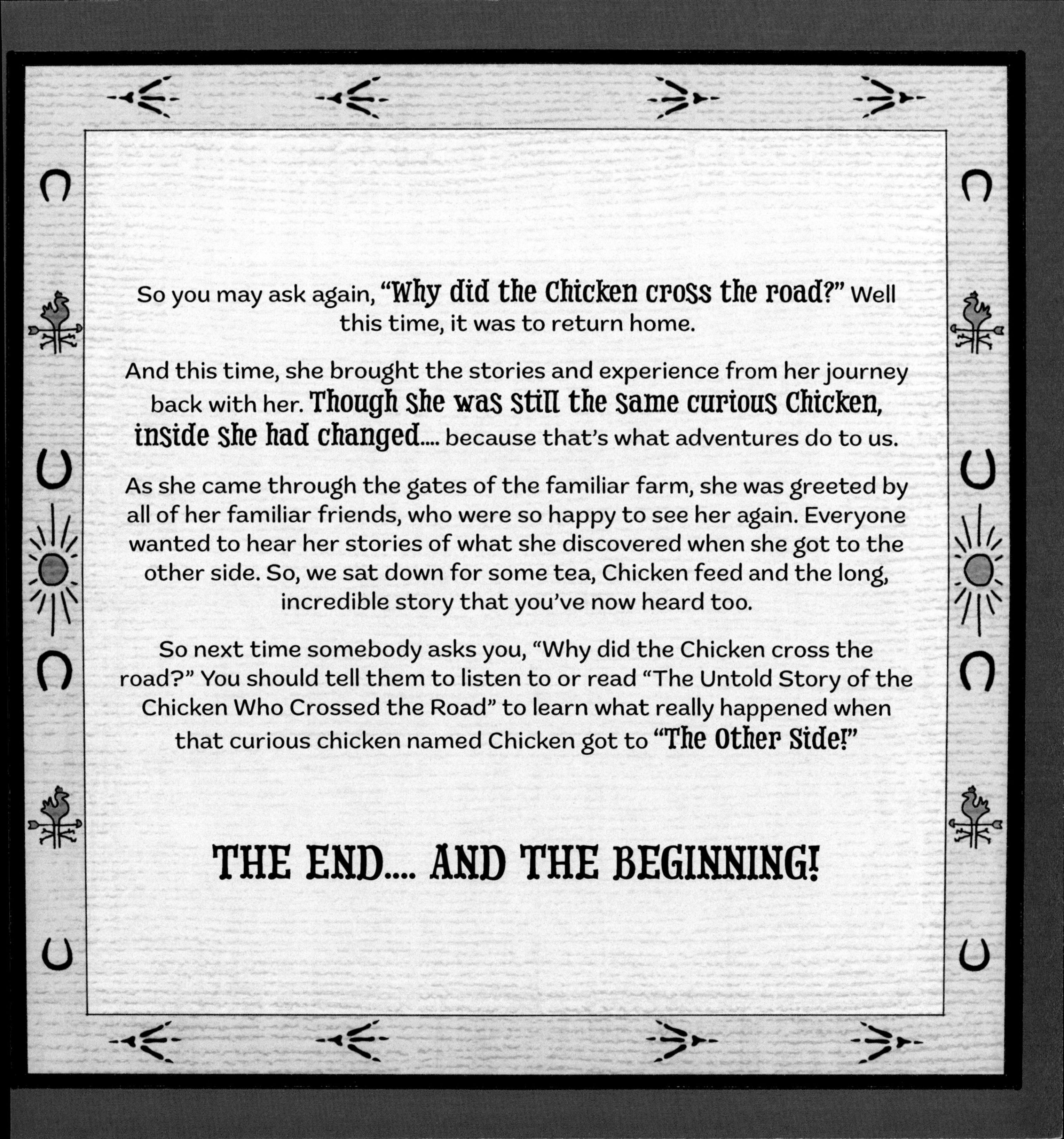

So you may ask again, "Why did the Chicken cross the road?" Well this time, it was to return home.

And this time, she brought the stories and experience from her journey back with her. Though she was still the same curious Chicken, inside she had changed.... because that's what adventures do to us.

As she came through the gates of the familiar farm, she was greeted by all of her familiar friends, who were so happy to see her again. Everyone wanted to hear her stories of what she discovered when she got to the other side. So, we sat down for some tea, Chicken feed and the long, incredible story that you've now heard too.

So next time somebody asks you, "Why did the Chicken cross the road?" You should tell them to listen to or read "The Untold Story of the Chicken Who Crossed the Road" to learn what really happened when that curious chicken named Chicken got to "The Other Side!"

THE END.... AND THE BEGINNING!

Join the majikkidsclub !

Be the first to hear our new stories & meditations, access our downloadable colouring books, get games, activities, cool conversation starters, discounts on books and other magical stuff that's fun for the whole family! Enjoy a sample of what's included in the Majik Kids Club in the following pages.

Visit us at majikkids.com !

Conversation Starters

Either share your answers to the questions with your family, friends or classmates OR write your answers on the lines below.

What did you admire or like most about the chicken named Chicken?

____

____

____

Why do you think Chicken had such an easy time making friends?

____

____

____

What are 3 things you are curious about and want to learn?

____

____

____

Help Chicken Return to The Farm

To listen to an audio version of this story and to find many more magical books, join the Majik Kids Club at majikkids.com!

Bradley T. Morris is the founder of Majik Kids. He is grateful to have built himself a career that allows him to write, produce and publish all sorts of media that primarily uses entertainment as a vehicle to teach, transform and inspire. He plays Professional Golf for fun.

Sauryn Majik Sauryn is five years old and has already co-authored six books with his papa bear, Bradley T. Morris. Sauryn is also a voice actor and the creative director at Majik Kids - helping us to write, produce and publish the most magical stories for all the magical kids around the world.

Amy Ebrahimian is a mixed practice artist who delights in creating artwork which sparks the imagination. She hopes that this offering entertains and uplifts you! To see more of her work, visit www.mehndinomadic.com.